JACQUELINE CIOFFA

GEORGIA PINE

Copyright © 2015 by Jacqueline Cioffa.

All rights reserved. No part of this book may be used or reproduced in any manner whatsoever without written permission except in the case of brief quotations embodied in critical articles and reviews.

This is a work of fiction. Names, characters, places and incidents either are products of the author's imagination or are used fictitiously. Any resemblance to actual events or locales or persons, living or dead, is entirely coincidental.

Cover image © Laura Makabresku.

This book was formatted and designed by:
Downtown Books Publishing
66 Genesee Street
Auburn, NY 13021
downtownbooksandcoffee.com/

ISBN 978-1-507-54920-9

To Magdalena de Los Angeles

Perspective

I wrote *The Vast Landscape*, the prequel to *Georgia Pine* at a dark, scary time in my life. Harrison, the brash heroine, was someone tangible I could cling to. She gave me reason to get up, to go on, to fight, a much-needed respite from what was happening in my real, everyday life. I made the conscious decision not to write about manic depression, the disease that has disrupted every neuron firing through my beautiful, chaotic mind. Bipolar Disorder, the label I detest, is *en Vogue*. It appears in trendy bestsellers, Oscar winning films and sensationalized television. It's glamorized, modernized, made to look *cool*. Trust me, it is not. Mental Illness is the train wreck, the ugly, cruel, exhaustive, intangible, and solitary battle. It does not discriminate among rich, poor, smart, stupid; it brings grown men to their knees, ripping whole families apart. Writing *The Vast Landscape* freed me to live my dreams on the page. Harrison is I, I am she, mixed together so deeply the lines disappear. The outlines blur, intentionally. Was *The Vast Landscape* reality or fantasy? That is for the reader to decide. We are all disabled, broken parts, lost individuals, trying to find our way. Truth is what you know, here and happening now. There is only love and love is the bravest character of all. Harrison is the voice in our heads, asking the important questions. Where do I fit? Why am I here? Will I love, be loved? We are born with a fixed expiration date, yet we carry on, walking this earth the best we can until we're pixie dust. Cherished, kept alive in memory and yellow parchment, we become precarious, aged photographs in a cardboard box. Lives touch, intersect in the most unpredictable yet meaningful ways. The essence continues because *you* do. Harrison leaves the door open a crack. I seize the opportunity to revisit my whole, healthy self a bit longer, live in the mystic beach home I adore, dream eyes open. Hope is our greatest asset. To choose hope against the worst possible odds is the true measure of life.

The story continues in… *Georgia Pine*.

GEORGIA PINE

One Two, Hut-Hut

She wills her eyes awake, dreading the long, agonizing night stretching before her. She is petrified of the dark, harrowing silence, night terrors, horrific dreams. She keeps her cell close in bed, reassurance she can reach the outside world. Pathetic, she knows. She won't use it when she wakes out of her mind, trapped, screaming in silence. She is alone for the first time. She misses Harrison so much that her toes ache, which is impossible. She has no lower limbs, no feeling below the groin since the magical age of five. The Biblical number meaning, "God's grace." Harry's wild adventures kept her alive. The loss of her mother and her life-supporting imaginary friend left no room for breath; the gaping abyss relentlessly pierced her acrid heart. The room was dark, save the iridescent blue hue from the nightlight. Miss Bossy Pants *aka* her nurse, left hours ago. She came twice a day per strict instructions in her mother's will. Even from oblivion, mom is barking orders. She was fine with self-induced confinement; isolation suited her. She had Harry living under her skin. The stories kept her alive, satiated, curious, anxious. Harrison gave her reason enough to stay. She typed away, the journeyman along for the ride. She was in perpetual movement, racing with her phantom limbs. Change thrust on her hadn't been factored in. Life-altering, earth shattering change left her unprepared, ill-suited for the monotonous shiteous task of living. The mother-daughter learning curve eviscerated, she was left without precious tools desperately needed. She discarded pen and paper; only pencils were allowed in her home. She hadn't bathed in weeks, brushed her teeth, washed her hair. She didn't feel like watching a film, eating dinner on a TV table or taking meds. She didn't feel. She wanted death. She begged God to take her. She was a coward, a shell inside an empty box consisting of blood, cells and water, worthless waste of oxygen. The pushy silver sun snuck through the pane blinding her, yet she was bone cold. Seasons turn no matter the measure of grief. 6:00 a.m. frost sat on the lawn while muted pumpkin, rust red and muddy brown leaves concealed dormant grass. How unbearably sad. She imagined how it felt, rising mist, brittle treetops, brisk air thievery seeping through the cracks of an aged, worn oak windowsill. Fall would be gone; the days would grow short. For her, the excruciating nights grew long. The alarm clock flashed bold, blood LED numbers, 7:45 am. Shit, Bossy Pants wouldn't show up until nine. An hour to ruminate; thinking was toxic. It did absolutely no good. She jerked the urinal bag, threw it on the untouched, day old dinner and fumbled for the grab bar, yanking herself up. At least she had slept through the night. Yes, there was that.

China Glaze and High Hopes

The doggy bell hanging from the backdoor knob chimed. Bossy Pants had a set of keys for obvious reasons. She let out a sigh, rolled her eyes anticipating the pert, chirpy intrusion. Any second she'd round the corner, all cheery and shit. The yellow mane perched high atop her head reminded her of a horsetail. Made her snicker every time. Crude, evil and mean-spirited, true bitterness took years to perfect. Bossy was pretty, not in a vulgar way but a homespun, organic one. She wasn't half bad, never pitied the client, pushed her hard. Her nurse's uniform consisted of Hane's sweatshirts, short shorts (even in winter), flip-flops and obscene red, sparkly toes. Twinkle toes, OPI nail polish, *China Glaze*.

"Morning sunshine, how'd it go?"

She shook her head, turning towards the wall despising the impending push and pull. Morning routine never deviated course. Bossy Pants pulled Tupperware from under the bed and began rounds.

"No good? You've got to eat sweetheart," says horsetail as she goes into the kitchen. She hears the faucet's steady stream, dishes clank in the sink. Ten minutes tops, she'd be back. She couldn't be *that* stupid, dreading her return.

"Front or back?"

"Front."

Morning exercises *oh joy*, wincing in pain for dramatic effect. She feels nada; Bossy does the heavy lifting as she counts.

"You reek. How about we go upstairs?"

"How 'bout you *go to hell*."

"Only if you go first." Cliché. She chuckles, kid's got spunk. Bossy hands her a 5 lb. dumbbell. Her arms are lean and muscular. Instantly transformed, she's Harry with gladiator arms. Strong, supple, action heroine, movie star biceps.

"Enough theatrics, on your back." She moans out loud.

"If you'd get up, we could avoid the drama."

"No." All she could see were those garish, slap in the face toes. Rubicund, yuck. What she would give to have her toes, ankles, kneecaps. She'd scale the Himalayas, walk miles and miles barefoot in the desert, dance in the surf, hike until the blisters turn callous. She'd grab a backpack and leave, unapologetic, the mighty warrior. She was grateful she couldn't feel the tube being shoved up her ass, *enema central*. Bossy wasn't horrible, she slept on the couch for months when her mom died, pressed a cool, soothing lavender washcloth against her forehead until the fever broke and wails subsided. Hell, she knew every inch of that broken body. She stuck it out. Bossy had been with her since she was a child. She was too heavy for her mom, hard to manage. She got sick a lot, weak, susceptible to all sorts of illnesses, a common cold could knock her on her ass for months. Her mom needed a nurse to administer shots, IVs, enemas. Bossy showed up with that nauseating perkiness. She was solid, on the right side of the bed across from her mom. They had a ritual, worked in tandem; sponge bath, dress, fed in under half an hour. When she was little, they giggled and made it a game; she timed them with a Raggedy Ann clock. When she got older, her broken body grew weaker. Every day was grueling. She didn't laugh anymore. Nothing was fun; life was not a game. Not hers, not anymore. She smashed the clock against the wall, shards of Raggedy Ann and childhood remains obliterated for good.

She escaped, lost in worlds she controlled. She wrote the second her mom fastened the tray to her chair, whittling the hours. Fantasy became more real than her miserable existence. She disappeared inside the land of make believe, filled with Crayola Crayons so bright she wore tinted sunglasses as she typed. She filled boxes and boxes with notebooks, fantasy, dragon slayers (*didn't take*), erotica (*too fake*), polar bear adventure (*too immature).*

On her eighteenth birthday, her mom surprised her with a brand spanking new, state of the art laptop. She'd seen the advertisements. She knew her care cost them any pleasures in life. Dad worked fulltime plus side jobs to keep his precious baby home. He wasn't around a lot, but boy did the house light up when he breezed through. He rarely missed bedtime smooches. He'd hop on the bed snuggling real close, recounting hilarious stories, grazing her forehead and promptly conking out. She missed his obnoxious snore, stolen sleepy time minutes, Old Spice overkill, spaghetti and meatballs, peppers and onions breath. He was *nothing* like her, had too many friends, family and neighbors. She loved their exclusive bond, he adored her, she never doubted him. Not ever, not even now. They were the boring, middle class family plus a gimp. She understood why her brothers hated her. She wasn't blind; she caught the sneers of resentment when they flew by, slamming the back door. She stole their mother's time and killed their father. Heart attack, barely fifty. X was destroyed, he worked so hard. She never stopped being sad, living with the guilt, missing every single thing about him, even the ridiculous pranks. She was sorry, so very, very sorry she would never see him; the atheist in her knew better. Still, she'd keep looking until her eyes closed, *for good*. She finally got a long, uninterrupted, blissful sleep. He wasn't there, waiting, sweet nothing was. It wasn't some magical dream dimension where she grew legs. It wasn't sad, not to be human. No messy emotion, no pain, no thoughts, no feeling. It was background noise, the constant hum of an air conditioner you hear, but scarcely notice.

And that was a blessing.

She almost dumped the chair, shrieking at the top of her lungs unwrapping the streamline, box shaped laptop. It would take years to transcribe her notes. She didn't care, had nothing *but* time. Boy, was she wrong. Time didn't stop, pity the cripple. She submitted 2,500 words, a 'life in the chair/day' essay, terrified of scrutiny. Much to her pessimistic chagrin, bad reviews never came. Published by eighteen, debut novel at twenty-five, the National Book Award for Fiction. Refusing interviews, the press dubbed her '*the eremite.*' They were right. Not one single photograph got leaked. That was easy; agoraphobics never leave the house. Medical checkups, doctor came to her. She kept life simple, didn't worry about buzz, PR, the blah, blah white noise. Made her mom proud, that mattered. She took over the bills. It couldn't erase the lean years, her dad's premature death. Still, it had to help. She hoped she was less of a burden, less pitiful. She was stupid rich, with nothing to spend it on. Ah, sweet and sour dumplings leave a bitter aftertaste on the tongue.

"If you don't get… I quit." She knew Bossy was serious by the crazed look in her eye. She got this intense squint when she was pissed. She looked possessed. It was kind of funny when she was little, not so today.

"Your mother would be disgusted. The house has been taken over by cardboard boxes, damn fan letters. Idiot. I'm not your fucking assistant or personal postman."

"Burn 'em." Crappers, she was livid. Bossy did not curse.

"Fine, spoiled brat. Toss the piss bag one more time; I'll make you drink it. Swear to God. I miss her too, selfish monster. She'd be furious. I'm done. You shower in the morning, up to you."

Bossy lifted her under the shoulders, hoisting her up, fluffing the pillows. She made scrambled eggs, wheat toast and left. How predictable.

"Here you go, high priestess. OJ, eggs and toast." Bossy storms out, slamming the door. She's in big trouble, shit storm trouble. The bells ring mad, chiming like a holy mother of God reborn, hallelujah, praise HIM Sunday choir.

Damn Straight

X tries to watch a movie, squander the looming hours. Six to be precise, before Bossy's imminent return. She can't get comfortable, back aches, shoulders tight, jaw clenched. Rolls her neck ten times in each direction, nada. Her mind was spinning in too many directions. She was freaking the fuck out. For the first time in months, she forgot about her mom. She panics, distraught. She despises the thought of a stranger in her house, much less a new nursemaid. She downs the disgusting, lukewarm eggs and half piece of toast, forcing the juice, guzzling water from the portable cooler. Combs her oily, stringy hair, ewe gross. Bossy was right, it was a knotty, grease-ball mess. Fuck, fuck, fuck you twinkle toes. She went too far. Her mother would've whooped her ass, yanking her out of bed so fast, giving her whiplash. The glaring, red numbers from the clock would not move. Each passing minute felt like poison ivy on a phantom toe she couldn't itch, time stuck. What would Harrison do? She'd put on a too-tight, black tank, hot leather pants, motorcycle boots and take off. Too messy for Harry, out the door, cussing and kicking dirt. She reached the trapeze overhead lifting her torso, whipping off her cozy, linen pajama top, putting on the predictable, pale blue, cotton button-down left on the bed. She needed new clothes, something trendy that looked tough. Bottoms never matter, it was hard to look sexy in diapers. She could buy anything, have anything, custom motorized chair, swanky, pimped out cripple van. *(yeah, catching herself. Her mom scolded, "can't say cripple outside this room, offensive.")*

She'd pack light. Head west, travel like Harry. Except, she was petrified. Couldn't make it to the front porch. Her mom tried coaxing, bribery when she was little. Pathetic twig of a thing would shake and scream. That street, she couldn't face it. Pebbles in the road, the curb, basketball net, neighborhood kids oblivious. They had no idea a bouncing ball could make her sob. *That* day played over and over in her twisted mind. She woke soaking, always the same disgusting, graphic nightmare. Awake, asleep, she never escaped in time. Everything feels brave when you're five. The snapping of bones, the gushing, bubbling, ruby red puddle, shredded veins dangling midair, summer swelter, melting tar, the crushing, crucifying sound of an 1100 lb. chrome bike as it pummeled her legs. She was spliced. Guts and roadkill, the dying animal in the street you close your eyes to avoid. She wasn't lucky; she wasn't dead. Only half of her went missing. She survived, forced to relive it like some kind of reverse therapy, leaving her more damaged than before. After a while, her mom quit. She couldn't bear, utterly helpless watching her paralytic child wail. If X ever did summon the courage to hightail it, there'd be IV's, shots, meds and pee bags to pack. She covered the piss bag with a blanket. Yeah, so not supermodel material. Insurmountable odds. She stared down the clock telekinetically willing the numbers to move. She was at the highway, halfway mark. Could she break free from the stifling, cracked espresso walls? Be the explorer, warrior, gypsy, nomad, high priestess, fierce heroine she created. The choice for *them* was simple, her not so much. It meant something else. Call *her* X, as in anonymous, without the annoying *X*mas carolers, twinkling bulbs, fake snow, dripping silver icicles, phony illusion. The blue spruce replaced by the practical, artificial one.

X, the name *Seven* gave her. The walled fortress kept the prisoner too comfortable.

X detested the required doctor visits, pious look of pity from a stranger. Her stumps were grotesque, her mind razor sharp. Fate was a spiteful bastard; late at night in the eerie stillness and shadow quiet, she wished that bike had squashed her head.

A child never notices the googly eyes. She loved being outdoors, fresh air, content in the chair for hours. Everything feels lighter in the sun. The neighborhood kids were pals; children don't see defects. They'd push her to the top of the street, whip her round and let go. She'd whiz past the blurred houses, beating the stupid boys on bikes. The wipeouts. X didn't care when she wound up on the neighbor's lawn. In flight for a split second, she was free. Until she tasted asphalt, bruised, bloodied, pieces of gravel embedded in her skin, war wounds. Someone noticed, eventually. Picked her up, put her back in the chair, wiped the blood with a dirty t-shirt and continued playing. When she was really lucky, she landed on soft, springy, un-mowed sponge grass. That was good a day, not a scratch. Her mother would never know. Yeah, that rarely happened.

"Again, with the antics? Someday you're going to get hurt," her mom retorts pushing X up the ramp inside the house. Instantly realizing the ridiculousness of the statement, wishing she could reel it back. X looked at her mother with so much disgust, it was more than she could bear. She popped a wheelie, did a 180 and stormed off. In that moment, contempt and hatred were born.

Summer fell short; the kids went back to school. She was stuck home with a tutor, nurse and nursemaid. X was growing up. The street kids no longer innocent, interested in her. Boys, cars, pinching Salem's, drinking Old Milwaukee behind the garage, spin the bottle was way cooler than the kid in a wheelchair. She saw how they looked, began covering her extremities. The pisser tube tucked and hidden, bag under her skirt. On good days, she wore pull-ons, damn bladder infections, most of the time forced to use the pee-bag. Just because she couldn't feel below the waist, she saw everything. She knew exactly what was happening.

"Gross, smell *that*?" X overhears the nasty, vicious ringleader. The pretty, popular girl; slut with double D's the boys tried to feel up. Curly brown, tight perm, mean girl ruled the street.

"It's *her*," pointing at X with repulsion. The kids snickered, ignoring X and scurrying away.

"So annoying."

X didn't flinch years later when she saw the half-paragraph obituary. The absurd high school picture, curly top died young. Mother of four, lived in a trailer park on the outskirts of town. Why do people do that, use outdated photographs? Nasty, hateful, jealous, ugly, envy festered bitch got breast cancer. Cancer puffers, crap genes and her twelve-pack a day beer habit, didn't help.

It's preposterous looking back, the moments that stick. The shortest sentences leave the deepest scars. X fled home in shame, forever changed; innocence, optimism and youth left at the curb.

Bedrock and Bedrails

Jingle bells. Lord hath mercy. X sits at attention, wringing her hands. Exhausted with worry, tossing and turning. Her mom would be so mad; demand better, stop acting like a brat.

She snuck a peak at the half empty bed, where her daughter's limbs were absent. It was her fault, she blamed herself for shooing her kids out the door. Just a little peace, quiet for a few hours. Besides, the air was good for them. Preoccupied with dinnertime, getting supper on the table 5:30 sharp. That's what her husband expected, X didn't get it. His home, his rules were all she knew. Familial obligation, tradition embedded in the walls. X didn't know her mom was planning to build a house, saving, nothing fancy. Modern appliances, freshly painted walls, furniture that was not tattered from years of abuse. A backyard to plant seeds, bulbs, vegetables, marveling each spring when the floral bonanza began to grow. After the accident, insurance, hospital bills, money was non-existent. Choice was a luxury her mom tossed. She washed mountains of laundry, went over homework, chores were easier without X underfoot. Her relentless curiosity, twenty questions, she couldn't pee with the door closed. They lived in a typical, small, rural town. She sent her kids outside after school, no matter the climate. That's what was done. She figured X was safe, kept one ear peeled on the street noise, fights, laughter, roars, bouncing basketballs. She could tell by the sounds, they were fine. If she'd only insisted, on a bigger, better-equipped hospital, one with state of the art triage. In shock, forced to make split second decisions, covered in her baby's blood. The doctors assured her, her daughter would have bled out. Crushed in half, she cheated death. Late at night lying in bed, eyes burning with exhaustion, she sobbed into her pillow. Her husband snored beside her; she listened enviously. She secretly wondered if it might've been better if her child had died on impact. She hated herself, it had been a particularly, grueling day. X had been X, extreme and obstinate. Not to mention her boys felt abandoned. There wasn't enough of her to go around.

"*Mom!*" X screamed, a thousand times a day.

Dutifully, she got up, rub her chaffed, crusty eyes and headed downstairs. She sat in the chair by the bed, lowered the handrail, smoothed the sheet, tucking her in snug. She stroked her hair and waited for X to fall asleep placing her head on the bed, dozing. Startled, she woke and glanced at the clock. 3:00 a.m. She straightened the sheets, stood over her beautiful, broken girl and raised the bedrail.

"I'm right upstairs. You're fine," she whispered more for her benefit than her child's. When she didn't come down by ten on a sunny Monday morning in June, X panicked. Her mom never slept late. She knew, phantom extremities frozen. She shivered soaking wet, the sheets soiled in urine from the overflowing bag. She was out of her mind, could not move. X could not get warm, on the balmy, 70 degree morning. She was gone. Death by sorrow and exhaustion, it was *her* fault. She couldn't lose Bossy too, not an option. Bossy Pants had a strange look on her face, envelope in hand. She sat on the bed and stroked X's hair.

"Looks nice." Bossy Pants waited, grinning.

"You can't leave. Please. It stinks in here. I need a shower. I'll do better," smugness wiped from her face, replaced with terror. She wiped a tear from her cheek.

"Wasn't planning on it. I had to do something, end the pity party of one. Besides, your mother would kill us." Bossy embraces X, she reciprocates, tension dissolves into the wrinkled, bed sheets. No matter how hard she tries, the memories keep her stuck. The first day coming to that home, the sight of the helpless, scared, maimed child with half a body. It was gruesome. X was hard to look at, and she was a trauma nurse. Seen the worst, or so she thought. Bossy had to leave the room, afraid she might burst into tears. Pity was the last thing the child needed. She knew she'd have to be stern. Bossy never displayed sympathy, but sadness lived on the walls of that room. Grown woman or not, a little girl was robbed of a whole life.

"Read this. Just the one; I'll deal with the rest." Bossy dangles the envelope, sparking curiosity.

"Front or back?"

"Front," X smirks defiantly.

"Front, alrighty then." Bossy lets out a sigh, grabs the Tupperware under the bed. Whistling her annoying, happy whistle, goes to the kitchen. Maybe, just maybe things could be different. Not wanting to jinx it, X stops. She doesn't dare think, much less say the word, aloud. Hope.

The Gene Pool

X could not wait for Bossy to get lost, now that she knew she wasn't leaving. She was the exemplary patient, without a hint of complaint. Bossy wasn't stupid, she knew what she was doing. X could not wait to open it. A letter, from a fan? She never read one, especially while Bossy was lurking, give her the satisfaction. Why this one, she wondered? What was so different, from a million others? Okay, not *millions*, swollen ego deflated back to reasonable. She was a gifted writer, awards backing the talent. She never imagined she'd write something anyone would want to read. Her desperate need to feel whole, found purpose in the words. Her sharp mind needed a way to soar, outside the mutilated body. She figured out early on she could become someone else on paper, whomever she dreamt, travel to places she'd never been, never see, live life on her terms. Even if it was within the confines of her imagination, the made up world of make believe gave her the freedom she desperately needed to go on. They say it takes, *'10,000 hours to reach the roads of greatness, become a master.'* X had the hours, figured she might as well make use of the empty time. She never dreamt someone out in the real world would listen. Apparently love, longing, tragedy, hope and despair are universal themes. Humans are made of flesh, blood, bones, mind and spirit. We are the fallibles, gone before we barely get the chance to start. X knew, she learned early. Fuck God, God isn't sitting around worrying. He's busy being a figment of some poor sucker's imagination.

Bourbon and Bluegrass

Dear Ma'am,

Sorry about that 'X', couldn't find an author's name. Hell, I'm not even sure you'll ever get this. You are a hard person to track down. That's cool. I dig mystery. Hey, thanks for writing such a kickass book. 'The Vast Landscape,' I mean. To clarify, I know you wrote a bunch. I loved that one. I'll get to the reasons why. I have to confess I haven't read the others. I have to pick and choose how I spend my money. That book is a home runner. Harrison is killer. She's exactly who I'd like to be. Smart, sassy, fresh, sticky sweet and vulnerable, all that gooey shit she tries to hide. I even went out, found a pair of second hand black boots with a few holes. I swear they changed my life. Got laid last week, first time. Too much? Anyways, thanks for making me feel brave. Harrison saved my life. Or what's left. I never knew my mother, wish I had. I hear stories from my Dad, how cool she was, an artist, feminist. They warned her not to have kids. She told them to suck it, got pregnant with me. I heard they call you, 'the recluse.' I respect that. The world sucks. People are idiots, out for themselves. Stupid smartphones, technology, waste of energy. Trust me, no one bothers to buy actual books these days. They're all like, "why, when I can download on my Kindle?" We don't have money for fancy gadgets. I found a used paperback copy at The Salvation Army. I loved the cover, man. Wicked, black and white artsy, combat boots, genius. (don't be mad I didn't buy new, times are tough). Boy, can you write. I won't bore you too long with my sob story. I'm sure you've read thousands of letters. I hear you don't write anymore, you're done. No way! You have to keep on writing. It matters. Harrison's strength, will and grit keep me going. I'm not mad you made her up, I'm sure you had your reasons. Makes me love her even more. Harry's the sweet-devil in everyone. That poor writer, the one without legs in the chair, man does that suck. Talk about crap luck. Hope you made her up. I tend to ramble when I get over excited. I just turned eighteen. World is my oyster, some fucked cliché. I love clichés, and I'm no writer. My life is a cliché. Back to my mom because that's where my story begins, and fizzles. She looked like Joan Jett, whom I adore, lived in a tiny studio in the west village in NYC. She had two roommates and a cat to keep away the mice, until she met my dad. A redneck, country boy from the bayou, visiting a cousin, could've been a GQ model, chiseled face and muscles from days working the farm. They met on Carmine St. and Sixth Avenue, literally rammed into each other. She almost fell flat on her tush, he caught her with one arm. She was pissed, until she looked up. She was a goner. The fling stuck, packed her one bag and moved South to Louisiana, never looked back. She knew she had the gene, thought she'd beat it. Huntington's. Refused to get tested, until she got pregnant. Took her fast, they only had twenty-four months together. She was dying, literally suffocating to death in hospice, me still in her belly. She looked at my dad and blinked. He knew what it meant; they talked about it. Save her baby. He gave the doctor a nod; it was what she wanted. The doctors got me out, seconds before she quit breathing. Guess she waited until she knew I was safe. In Louisiana, farm life is ruthless. Gutted her like a pig, least that's how I imagine it. Daddy named me Opal Jett, after his wife and her idol, people around here call me Seven 'cuz I was early, born at seven months. My dad had lots of family to help with the raising. He never remarried, says true love only comes around once. For my eighteenth birthday, instead of presents, I got tested. I won't open the envelope, the results. I kind of need to know what's going to happen to Harrison's family first, Zack, Addie, her girls. I want to travel, do the brave things she did. I'm no model, tried to enlist. Army. Boats make me seasick. I suppose I'm asking you to finish the story. So I have a roadmap how to start living, before I start dying. I don't want to know how much there's left. Figure it's best to live it. Harrison stuck, can't shake her. Don't much want to. Be nice to have some kickass adventures, some hope. Thanks for making Harrison badass.

Bye now.
All ya'all,
Seven

Rawhide Whiskers

X must have re-read the letter fifty times. Heat rose inside out, making her wet. She envisioned swampland, mossy bayou, a green so vibrant she can't describe the magnificent beauty. Massive cypress, musk smell, painstakingly slow moving, gator-filled muddy waters. X wonders if Seven explores the swamps, passing time catching crayfish. She envisions a young girl, wholesome, plain enough with fine, mousy brown hair and dull, mud brown eyes, taped wire rimmed glasses, wearing frayed, faded jean shorts, ripped, Clorox stained, yellow-white camisole and beat up, black motorcycle boots. Seven sits crossed legged on the dirty, worn gray carpet at the one library in town. It's cool inside, damp and quiet, nobody bothers her. The librarian calls her by name, doesn't need to show a card. Engrossed in her books, she studies faraway places she dreams of, ones she'll probably never visit. Is the farmhouse a rusty, old aluminum shack? Inherited from long-dead settlers, southern ancestors, spirits of generations past, that had nothing but burlap sacks and a change of clothes. No leisure time, no currency to disguise rundown appearances. They woke to the dark, worked the fields, hands bloodied and raw, ate one meal come dinnertime, survived on sweet potato pie, corn husks, chicken and crabbies, whatever the bayou and bounty provided. Baths came Saturdays in washtubs sharing the same dirty water, heated with pans on the cast iron stove. Splintered, plywood floorboards gave away each step, random rusty nails sprung up, got hammered back down.

The wood trilled and moaned, frozen under bare feet. One rudimentary outhouse sat straight off the kitchen. Barbed wire kept the livestock in, grazing under a scorching Cajun, noonday sun. The animals stuck around, too overheated and tired to run.

Does her daddy look like Paul Newman? Is his face rugged, brown, tan skin weathered by the cracks of hard living? A stick of wheat dangling perpetually from his strong mouth, jaw clenched. How could *this* kid mean anything? She didn't know her, wasn't pissed about the invalid crack. She had that coming, shitty attitude and all. X googled Huntington's *'brain waste away'* disease. Fucking hardcore. You choke to death, can't catch a breath, lose all muscle control. *Waste away*, a slow, miserable, agonizing death. She'd rather be run over by a two-ton motorcycle, limbs shredded. X had her mind; that was something. Crap, what was *this*? What exactly was she feeling? Guilt? Remorse? She wasn't sure. Stupid, selfish, hip-tee-do mother. She knew the odds, got knocked up anyway. Did she really think she'd beat it? What about the dad? Was he ignorant, blind sighted by the mysterious, cool chick from the big city, or was he some ass-wipe hillbilly, thinking with his cock? She couldn't know, Seven didn't speak ill about them. For the first time she felt sorry for someone else. Somebody other than her. Wow, that was huge. Wavering, she didn't know what to feel, if she could help. X phoned Bossy, asked if she'd come early. She'd go bonkers without someone to mull it over. It was Bossy's fault, damn fool. Why couldn't she leave her be, mean and miserable. She wanted her mother. She wanted to go. She wanted to be anywhere, but in that room. She needed to get up.

Migrant Mother

X tries to grasp how a mother could be so reckless. She doesn't get it, her brain can't comprehend the risk, playing Russian roulette with a life. Fine, if it's yours. Go ahead, cut your hair in a mullet, smoke dope, drop acid, LSD, read the beat books. *On The Road*, her mantra. Listen to the groovy words in underground, NYC downtown basements, radicals fighting for change through poetry, justice in *AMERICA*, wearing nonconformist clothes. Smoke, rolled tobacco, peace protests, answer to none. The mysterious, migrant mother wears kohl eyeliner, black skinny jeans. Chain-smokes Lucky Strikes, dangling from an antique, jade and wood cigarette holder, five dollar flea market find. She has pickup sex, shacks up with a guy, then a girl. Whatever, free will, that's cool. Doesn't shave her pits, legs, lets her pubes grow long and wild. But, she was nothing like that, her *other* ego. She was a runaway, from a well-to-do family. The respectable home with green shutters, massive white columns, floral pattern furniture and impeccable, landscaped yard. She came from Connecticut, blue blood horse stock, old money and manor, fine pedigree. She was a good girl, made honor roll, all A's, a cheerleader, popular with the in-crowd. She had a steady beau through high school, gave her his varsity ring and stole her virginity.

It was June, summer was lazy, high school over. The air skin sticky, the cool breeze made the evenings bearable. She finished her three-course celebratory meal, lentil soup, lamb and organic

Jacqueline Cioffa

green beans picked from the garden and homemade, peach cobbler. Sitting on the screen porch with her parents, belly happy, drinking ice coffee feeling grownup. She wished they'd hurry already, get the "We're so proud speech over." She was missing Friday night fun at the drive in. She couldn't remember which film was playing, Benjamin was swinging by at dusk. In his new toy, the Popsicle cherry, Chevy Impala convertible, graduation gift from the folks. Ben had nice folks. The gang would be green. She couldn't stop squirming in the chair.

"Lizzie, sit still for Christ's sake." Oh shit, her mother never swore. Her mom was worked up, dotting her face with a lavender, lace embroidered hankie. She couldn't look at her pride and joy. They only had the one child. Liz never asked, she didn't mind. She liked being spoiled; suited her. Her father and mother needed to talk, it was important. Her mom wasn't her composed, proper self. The air grew thick; Liz had a crick in her neck, muscles ached. She felt clammy, she wasn't sick. She couldn't place it, the discomfort. Her dad was calm, patiently tried to explain mom was sick. He could barely speak; spit it out. She was dying. They didn't know much about the illness, Huntington's. They were going to New York, there was a doctor doing cutting edge research. Agreed to add her to the trial, bet her dad bought half the hospital. Liz would have to be tested; she might be a carrier. Suddenly, the crickets chirping became deafening. The only sound she could make out, her father's muffled voice drowned by the unremitting buzzing.

"So, sweet pea you'll come to the city. Elizabeth, did you hear me?"

Stop the white noise; the relentlessness grew deafening. She actually swatted her head, covering her ears. She might be going mad. Those were the last words she'd ever hear from her parents. Liz stood, adjusted her demure, off the shoulder, fuchsia petal silk dress, calmly walked to her sobbing mother, kissed her cheek, and bolted. "Hope you feel better, mother. Ben's coming, can't be late."

She stormed the stairs to her room, ran into her teal canopy sanctuary and flopped on the bed, trying to catch her breath, hanging her head off the side. She spots the stowed suitcases under the bed, and knows. Opening drawers, she throws random cloths, undergarments, socks, shoes and her toiletry bag in the suitcase. She lifts the music box with the dancing ballerina, exposing a felt bottom and $1,000.00. Graduation gift, *thanks* Grandfather and Gramma. It would run out fast, she'd have to be careful. Get a job. She heard the horn, peeled back the curtain, and there he was. Lucky boy, Benjamin the third. Her grammar school crush, first everything. Sporting a smart, crew cut, iron button-down and khakis, brand new Chevy. Waving at her like a retard, grinning goof. Poor thing, she only felt half sad, consumed with rage, betrayal. Liz was in denial, her parent's admission made no sense. Why did they have to tell? She might die and Ben was off to college, a bright, peachy future. That peach cobbler scorched the back of her throat, she might hurl. Not in the car, Liz. He'd meet some bubbly, demure girl from a proper family in no time. Ben didn't like to be alone. He slept with a nightlight.

"Sweet ride. Change of plans, take me to the train station."

Stupid boy did whatever she asked. He was the gold-Ben, and she was his girl. She had to *go*, wasn't going to sit there and watch her mother die. She went a little nuts, so what. Liz planned on cramming in as much living as she could. Ben wrote, she gave him *(and only him)* her P.O. box. Her mother died, gone in months. She was relieved she went fast. Liz was pissed. At both of them, they should have told her sooner. Maybe, it was better this way. She had the letter in hand, fuming, preoccupied, late for work at the coffee house, didn't bother to look up. Intent on where she was going. Bam. She rammed right into him, catching her off guard. She couldn't help herself, falling in love.

She knew the risks, loved him anyway. Maybe she wasn't a carrier, he was worth seven minutes of sunlight. When Seven was born, Liz used her last breath to hear her cry. She knew what was coming, and forgot. So in love with her child, she stopped being angry at her parents, God. She understood. She would die, Seven on her chest. As her spirit hovered, her poor husband slumped over her lifeless body and a tiny creature screamed, flailing little arms. Opal, Elizabeth's life purpose cradled in her daddy's arms, sobbing, rocking back and forth. Lizzie chose only one name, strong, traditional. In her heart, she knew her baby was a girl. She made her husband promise. He laughed, held her, tickled her cheek with his whiskers and whispered playfully, "what if *she's* a boy?" Liz shook her head defiantly, brushing him off. "She's not, she's Opal." He looked at his glowing wife, who gave up so much. Of course, he'd do anything she asked. He nodded, not knowing what lay ahead, except new life and possible death. Elizabeth had never lied to him, only to herself.

"*Opal. The name, Opal. An American baby name, meaning: Jewel. People with this name have a deep inner need for quiet, and a desire to understand and analyze the world they live in, and to learn the deeper truths.*"

Opal. Fuck man, that's exactly how X pictured her, and her parents. The mom wasn't so bad, at least not *this* woman. She chose hope and new beginnings in the face of debilitating illness. A guaranteed death sentence, Elizabeth chose *life*. The unborn child she would die for, Opal would live.

X wished she was that brave. If someone told her she would have a baby that would die a miserable death, would she go through with it? Carry the child with selfless love, without pause. Opal's mother was human, stumbling her way through the mess.

Seven Shades of Heaven

X called Bossy back, asked her to stop at Best Buy on her way. Buy one of those fancy Macbooks, Airbook the lightest. She wanted something portable. Hers was outdated, a dinosaur by tech standards. She had placed the order over the phone, under her name. *Yes Bossy*, her real name, not the pen name. It took eight months, between sponge baths, watching films, surfing the net to write and finish *The Vast Landscape*.

She wasn't really trying, wrote two hours a day. She'd better get typing, Seven was waiting. Who knew how much time, if she even had Huntington's. Didn't matter, X was of no use lying in bed all day. If she couldn't be dead, she better do something. The only thing she was remotely good at was writing. Well, at least that's what '*they*' said. The peanut gallery, mom, the awards, and the readers. She was blessed, she reckoned. Her life never felt like luck at all. She was a real shit, here was a young girl with more gumption. I bet I can write the sequel in seven, six months tops if I'm hauling. Bossy will have to get in touch with the girl, find her and let her know. *Opal, huh?* Funny name, kind of old school.

Where to start? Harrison, *help*. How are they? Lord knows I'm not well without you, your pain in the ass, smarmy attitude. I miss you, us, our adventures, the razor tongue. I miss Zack, wonder how he's making out. I even miss your brat, surfer sea goddess girl, Addie. Yeah, no, sorry, she's *so* not perfect. I understand she's your bronze angel, not like us. You spoil her, made it easy. I made it easy, figured you suffered enough.

It's late, my eyes have gone fuzzy and I'm grumpy. Bossy should be here with the new laptop and food. I'm starving, for once. That's enough, for the both of us. Imagine, naming a little girl Opal? Sounds kind of awful. Harry, do you think other people talk to (*make believe*) people in their heads? Like me? I'm having a conversation with an imaginary, dead person. Who's made me stupid rich, thank you very much Harrison. It's good to have you back. I promise to go easy on them, your descendants. The cast of bizarre characters is shaping up. Georgia's about the same age you were when you split. She has her grandmother's naughty ways, but the kindest, loyal heart. She's one hundred percent, pure, clean oxygen, with a hot-head temper. She's part Adelaide too, stares at the horizon for hours, dreaming secrets she'll never share. Zack's all right, he's Zack. Your granddaughters' idolize him. I have a witchy feeling you already know that. Georgia spends summer breaks at the Cove. She wants to get away from her annoying sisters, space, quiet. The brats follow her everywhere. The twins, Zelda and Gertrude, got involved in sports, have to be dragged to Cali. They lost interest in the Cove, as tweens do. Maxine, she adores the Cove, says it feels better than home. She's an odd child, spends her days reading, swimming, collecting shells, colored glass washed ashore. When Georgia pokes or teases her, Maxine's lips curl. Pitiful, Georgia feels guilty. Zack is stern, scolding Georgia. Warns her to leave Max be, she's different. It's the only time Georgia recalls her grandfather raising his voice. Made her cry, sea salt tears.

Tomorrow Harry? I type, you listen. I knew you wouldn't go far. There's a whole universe filled with dust pockets and invisible colors, only visible through man-made telescopes. From 50,000 ft. in Chile, ALMA rotates, discovers what you now know. The beginning of time unveiled, back to the first moments after the universe was formed. Life was happening before, above, below and encircling the planet. Dust particles form colors so magical, invisible to the human eye.

One Times Four

The Cove, there was no other place Georgia wanted to be. She loved summers at the beach with her pops. Georgia pulled the rocker close to her grandfather's, almost touching. She needed to be near, reassured by the sounds of his breathing. Side by side, gliding back and forth. She had nowhere to go, nowhere she'd rather be. Mostly, she rocked while he nodded off. He was her most favorite person. She refused a life without him. Georgia knew what was coming. Maxine wasn't the only one with a gift, she didn't brag. Her grandmother was a fading memory, but Georgia could still recall the tight squeeze of her hand. How overtired giggly they got when she tucked her in. Harry whispered secrets in her ear.

Don't let anyone make fun of you carrot top, freckle face, how you are. Someday, they will see how dazzling and pretty you are. Stand your ground, find something to believe in and go for it. Don't look back. Don't apologize. Be nicer to your mother, she was a free spirit once. She plain forgot. Make her laugh when she gets too serious. Protect and cherish your sisters, they're what you got. At some point, you will be disappointed by them, even hate one or all. They might despise you, too. It won't matter, your sisters will pick your side every time. I promise, that's what families do. Your family, our family is bound by deep love and tradition. We are not quitters; we are backwards optimists. Takes a little longer, we get there on our time. I love that shared trait. We believe in our truths, once we've ripped them apart and examined the guts with a loupe. I'm dying baby, I won't spare you, hide the truth. You won't have to wonder where the hell I went. I adore you too much to leave you questioning my invisible parts. I love you right now, in this room, on this bed. You're my big girl, so smart. I will miss bedtime tuck-ins, our secrets. Don't tell your mama, she won't understand. You have your grandfather's eyes, and my cautious curiosity. Close your tired eyes, tomorrow we'll go to the beach. Hug your grandfather when he gets sad. He'll need you Georgia Pine, when I go.

Georgia looks at Harry through the puzzled eyes of an eight year old. Hush don't be afraid, life is about coming and going.

Georgia checks her grandfather who was sound asleep, mouth open. Content, relieved he's sitting next to her and not Harry. She remembers her grandmother's voice, the face out of focus. Z-Z and Trudy were clueless, played dolls and traded outfits. Everyone loved the *twice blessed*, petite, delicate flowers. Bullshit, they were annoying and she was glad they stayed in Maine. She went a little nuts, hung with the wrong crowd. Smoked dope, snorted coke and tried heroine, once. When the cops caught her selling a dime bag of marijuana on school grounds, she got expelled.

Adelaide and Caden were shell-shocked, livid, at a complete loss. They provided a loving, supportive home in Maine, the girls seemed happy. Sure they had ups and downs, like families do. The raging hormones, periods, fights over boys, kid stuff. But this, they were ill-equipped to handle Georgia. Addie secretly wished for sons. Girls, girls and more girls; over emotional, royal pains in the ass. She could picture her mother's smug look, taunting her. Addie grabbed the Tequila atop the kitchen cabinet, dusted it off, opened the cap and poured a shot. She offered Caden the bottle, he declined and caressed her cheek. Adelaide's lips forced a smile. "She's going to be fine babe, growing pains." Adelaide's mouth grazed the back of his hand. She wasn't so sure.

"Night, don't stay up all night. Hangovers and teenagers are the pits." Caden winked, left Addie alone in the kitchen, bottle of Tequila and shot glass in hand. Although he knew it wasn't the brightest idea, he'd learned the hard way. Best leave her be.

Georgia was too much like her grandmother, she had the devil riding a pinch above her right shoulder. She acted out, screaming silently. Georgia had no idea *who* she was, what they expected, she was lost. She was a runner, loner, kept the pain inside. She'd turn sixteen soon. Addie felt pangs of guilt. She'd been overwhelmed with the twins, did she give Georgia enough time, affection? How could she with Trudy, and Z-Z tag timing her boobs. Max tugging her leg, projectile vomit, fevers, delirium in rotation was way too much. Georgia gave up calling for her, her baby for all of ten seconds. Caden was the solid one. Bath time, bedtime stories, kisses and hugs from his glowing monster, tucking her in every night. Even Zack spent more time with her firstborn. Adelaide got pregnant with Maxine immediately after Georgia. When Harrison died, Zack spent months at the Cove, alone, not showering, not eating. Addie called every day as promised, begging him to come to Maine. Last resort, Addie flew Georgia out, to keep him company. She was eight, way too young to fly alone. She let her go, despite her worry. Zack was thrilled. He took Georgia on long walks, swims, hikes, ice-cream, playtime on the swing set. Georgia reminded Zack of Harrison, Addie saw his face light up, whenever she ran from the sea into the waiting towel and wide-open arms. She was his precious ginger. Adelaide came to collect her, bring her home to Maine. Georgia pitched a fit, Zack promised he'd visit. She could come every summer. Adelaide couldn't believe eight summers had passed. Her baby girl was a distant memory. She thought about keeping the trust, a while longer. She knew once she gave Georgia the envelope, she'd be gone.

"Send her to Pretty, he's waiting." Addie heard Harrison whisper. Pretty was her nickname for Zack. Feisty Georgia Pine,

always yearning for somewhere else. I swear we wear the same heartache and black beating sinkhole. Georgia's just like Harrison; reckless youth made Addie squirm. She heard all about her mother's crazy escapades from Katia and Sophia, Harrison's best friends. Harry's arrogant, brazen, wild nature masked her true beauty, hiding the purest, truest, kindest heart.

"A gentle hand and firm guidance." Addie swore her mom was sitting at the table, doing shots, resting a heavy hand upon her shoulder. It must be the 100 proof, reaching up to meet her mother's hand, finding warm, dainty fingers in the dark. She jumps, stumbles and swings around. Maxine. Standing in her floor length, gray polka dot, flannel nightgown. Wispy, shoulder length, white hair made a halo, illuminating her head. Skin so pale, she's virtually transparent. Max might be a ghost, she should send the poor thing outdoors, Vitamin D deficient for sure. Addie releases her breath, unaware she's holding it. "Be Jesus, you scared the shit out of me."

"Language. The lady was here. She told me to give you a tight, bear hug and that you'd hate it. She said, *"send her to pops, for the love of Christ."*

"MAX!"

"Verbatim," Maxine hugs her mother counting to ten, turns and exits, satisfied. Maxine disappears as creepily as she'd crept in. Addie adored her daughters. But that child was something else. Compared to Max, Georgia was a slice of rhubarb pie smothered in warm, vanilla ice cream. Adelaide pours one more shot, slings it and wipes her mouth, licking the back of her hand. The shot stings, an I'm alive reminder, a good sting. Thank heavens Z-Z and Trudy were no trouble, no trouble at all. *"Give 'em time, sweet girl. Give 'em time."* Adelaide ignores her dead mother's voice, oozing sarcasm. She pushes her chair, stands woozy. Dizzy, the room spins, she grabs the table for balance. "Fuck off, mother." Adelaide walks to the sink, turns on the faucet and opens a bottle of aspirin, pops two. Doctor daddy's orders, she grins. She fills the glass under the cold tap, and guzzles. The water tastes amazing, like it came straight from the Antarctic Icecap. Why are the women in this family so goddamn infuriating? Okay Daddy, loud and clear. She's yours, for another summer.

Catch a Ride

Zack washes the linens in the guest room, straightens the kitchen, vacuums and scrubs the bathroom. Normally, Addie saw to the upkeep of the Cove, hired a housekeeper to come once a week, do light shopping and laundry. Zack grumbled, it was just him. There wasn't a mess, she needn't make such a fuss. Besides, as a doctor he still went to the hospital, two days a week. Had to keep busy, Addie knew it was more than that. He missed Harrison, never remarried. He'd shake his head, if you asked, he'd blow it off. "Ridiculous." Seventy, and still riding his bike. Adelaide always gave Pretty the same answer, "I promised."

Zack understood immediately, Harrison left specific instructions before her death. She had months to plot it out. She knew their daughter would carry them out, to the letter. Addie became the deluxe planner when the kids came. She kept a day planner, chalkboard calendar full of the girls' schedules, play dates, activities. Harry laughed. Blackberry never left her side. Sometimes Zack missed his carefree, beach loving, funny fish, surfer girl. What had this uptight, lunatic done with his daughter? When he looked at the stunning, competent, slightly paranoid, overly serious mother and wife, he searched for traces of his free-spirited and impulsive daughter. Every so often, when she wasn't aware anyone was watching, he caught a glimpse of her. The blond, sea-swept locks, giddy girl, being tossed into the ocean by her mother, resplendent. Harry could swing her daughter around for hours, never tiring of the repetition. He wondered why her arms never gave out, strong biceps from decades of working out. Pretty tried to cut Harry a break, Adelaide screamed for her mother. It was one of his favorite, vivid memories. Pure joy, unfiltered happiness. The day came too fast, too soon when Addie *hated* her mother. At least she thought she did, not so sweet sixteen. Harry was the most disgusting person on the earth, stupid, ugly and mean. Slamming doors, shouting matches, both in tears. Zack was the shield, safeguard between the storms, Harry and Adelaide's tirade. He taught Addie to surf, love the ocean, convinced Harry to loosen the reigns. That was rough, no mother wants to let go. There were hushed voices, heated arguments; Zack and Harry rarely fought. Harry caved eventually; she knew Zack was right.

Georgia was drowning inside trying to find her way out, just like her gypsy mother and grandmother. Never mind the reckless, stupid things she'd done. People can change if they are shown something different. Zack saw the good in everyone, drove Harry bonkers. He knew time was fading, she was barely getting started. Georgia would be eighteen in an earshot. Harry kept calling. Zack was almost ready, not quite. He had one more important job to do. It was vital, their summer together. Georgia would leave him, or he would leave her. Zack was banking on the first option. Dying is the body and mind's natural process, hard only on the ones left behind with a blanket of memories, sorrow, and insoluble questions.

Zack dug up Harry's flowerbeds, laid down huge tarps. He threw away decades of bounty, perennials, jasmine, saucer magnolia, peonies and exotic flora he couldn't name. Dutifully, he came out at dusk, turned the sprinkler system on. He sat on the porch, watched the coastal sky turn orange, pink and violet as the sun dipped behind misty gray waters. In the past neighbors would return from the beach, give him a wave and leave him in peace. "Looking good, Zack," they'd remark, admiring Harry's plentiful array of flowers. Harrison's perennials nearly drove her nuts; refused to grow. Zack told her to be patient, she wanted to kill the son of a bitch. Got her knocked up, ended her career, ruined her life. Not even remotely, she got the exact life she wished for. He began ripping them up with fervor. Without whispering in his ear, Harry knew exactly what Zack was up to. Georgia Pine. He had a plan, he'd tell her they died from a nasty fungus. Of course, she'd help. He was too old to be on his knees, digging in the dirt. It would be their special something, a project she could grow with her hands, nurture. It would be her gift, and Harry's. The memories of her grandmother waning, she remembered her smell, fresh cut flowers, dirt and sea, towering above her, the soothing, repetitive caress as she stroked her flaming hair, whispering secrets snuggled in bed.

You will do plenty, try lots of things, live many lives, you are unique, strong, your mother's gift to pops and me. Don't hate her too much, your mother was the most glorious, free spirit. Remind her how freedom feels. She won't forgive me for leaving; you will be the bridge between us. Georgia, you will hold this family tight, keep them together. Remember, these words mean nothing now, but someday when you've lost your way, they will find you, carry you home. You are capable, timeless green calcite, braver than your sisters. I have to leave, that's how it goes. I'm entrusting you, sweet Georgia Pine. With the house, this family. You are the gatekeeper now, the fixer. We are born with a sole purpose. With unique gifts, I suppose. We must decide whether to use them, or discard them. I know, I know, big words for a small girl. Georgia purses her lips and pouts. "I'm not little." Harrison smiles, preparing her for the days ahead. Tragedy does not discriminate. Distraught, dying and helpless, she won't be there. That was the thing, she wouldn't be there with them.

Zack spotted Georgia, before she saw the blue Prius. The way the sun illuminated her blazing hair, black rims, long, eggplant tie-dyed dress, Birkenstocks and that damn, torn leather backpack, his heart sped. She was a rough diamond, blinding and raw like Harrison. The fiery, long locks and way she moved was Adelaide, twenty years past. She was young, awkward, sharp, a clarity all her own. Harry sobbed and sobbed went they sent Addie away. He laughed, told her she was being silly, he understood better now. Adelaide turned eighteen, lost to them for good, the theatrics. He wondered did Harry know what was coming? He made too many airport drop offs and pick-ups, his fragile heart couldn't take much more. When Georgia caught sight of her grandfather, her eyes beamed, she waved like a lunatic, hurrying her gait. He was her person.

"Thanks for saving me from the shrew."

"That shrew loves you, young lady. What the hell is that?" Zack glances at her exposed skin. Georgia had a black orchid tattoo covering her left shoulder, bright pink streaks in her hair. She pulled her cardigan, twisted her hair hiding the color and shrunk low in the seat.

Zack was thrilled she liked flowers, pleased with himself. She'd be spending plenty of hours digging in the earth. The plan was simple; sheer exhaustion. Work her hard, wear down the teenage demons. Zack's knees were fine. His granddaughter was not.

Black Coffee

Life without her. Zack takes his coffee black most days. An old man, purple veins run down his arms and hands spotted brown from age, the dead giveaway. His brown hair and shadow beard peppered white, dazzling hazel eyes lacked the vibrancy they once had, whenever *she* was in close proximity. The house, their weathered, clapboard cottage by the beach with chipped, green paint, and a porch that could use staining. Adelaide took care of the details. Zack counted backward, the day he lifted his arms high, opened the cardboard box and set his love free. Harry caught a ride on a warm, soft breeze, not before enveloping him with her love. He knew his time was close. He could not wait one more second to get to her. The Cove never felt the same. Addie juggled her busy schedule, between him and her new family, it could not have been easy. She was a wonderful daughter. She did precisely what her dying mother asked, expected, and then some. Summers were reserved for Zack. Six weeks at the beach, the girls descended with princess carry ons, pink polka dot bikinis, striped hats and moody personalities. His dollies immersed in Adelaide and Harrison's world. Zack taught the twins to swim, hold their breath underwater, snorkel. Georgia loved to fish, surf and developed a passion for the ocean, like her mom. Maxine loved the water, careful not to burn. Her chalky, white skin transparent. Max set up base camp near the rocks. She didn't mind being separated from the group, liked the solitude away from her sisters. Her cheap dime store umbrella, books, thermos of filtered water, Sunscreen SPF50 waterproof kept her content. As soon as the sun was a sliver on the horizon she'd pack, begin the trek up the rocks, counting each step. There were seventy-four, maybe seventy-five, she couldn't be sure when the lady talked in her ear, so distracting. Some days she skipped a step, throwing off her count. There was always tomorrow, accompanied by the grand lady of the house. She loved dusk, faded purples, oranges and reds swirled signaling the magic hour when the spirit of Harry would appear. They'd chit-chat, who was she kidding, her grandmother did all the talking. Third degree, felt like the Harrison inquisition. Max didn't mind, she wanted to know about her. The lady was a busybody, forced Maxine to listen. She chose her, came to her. "Max, chop-chop, baby girl. Supper, time to set the table." If that child had not come out of her vagina, Addie would swear she was a stranger. So peculiar, Blue Agave nectar. Zack grilled the catch of the day, Georgia flipped her hair, stomping a foot, making a stink.

"Smells gross, I'm not eating *that*." Zack was fully prepared for the onslaught of culinary diversity from his granddaughters. Hamburgers and Hoffman hots on standby in the cooler. Didn't stop him from trying. Georgia loved burgers and corn on the cob, defiant like her grandmother. Zack loved her headstrong ways and pouty, freckle face. She made him laugh, out loud. She reminded him most of his beloved, all that was missing. He almost forgot Harry when Georgia was around. Maxine, the effervescent, pensive child, proclaimed her independence quietly and fervently. She despised her name. It was boring and stupid. She wanted to be called Fallon. Addie looked at her dad, rolled her eyes and shook her head. She learned early which battles to pick.

"Fallon? Maxine is such a pretty name." Addie giggled, covering her hands over her mouth.

"Yes, mama. Fallon or Harry. The pretty lady suggested," pointing towards the house. Adelaide felt sick. She knew her mother wasn't gone, she'd never leave Pretty behind. One minute a chill ran up her neck, the next she was boiling. Typical, make up your mind mother. So now she was messing with Max, her seven year old. Maxine was an identical mini-Addie, minus the blond, curly locks and wise remarks. Her hair was paper thin, like her lean, ballerina body, skin almost see-through. She had hypnotic, aquamarine eyes. Maxine was delicate and thoughtful, a rare, precious sea urchin. Max lived in the ocean, came out pruny and giggly, an old soul. Addie bribed her to come out. She was too little to remember her grandmother, but man she adored pop. She threw a tantrum when it was time to go home, to Maine. Kicking and screaming on the kitchen floor, painful to watch.

"Mama, he'll be all alone, he can't *hear* her," barely audible through wails. Nothing consoled her. She didn't want to leave him and the bald lady. Nobody mentioned her grandmother went bald. Harrison refused to have pictures taken when she was sick. Maxine, her intuitive child, equal parts human and enchantress. Not witchy, God no, she was too kind to be mean. Addie couldn't be sure, she suspected her mom had a sixth sense. Guess Maxine, *aka* Fallon, had more of her mother than she thought. No matter how far the heart strays, you never escape the beginnings. Her parents, who birthed, shaped and provided a safe, loving magical home by the beach, worshipped her. Guiding the descendants, from a faraway place we don't understand, only visit in dreams. Sometimes, the hints are subtle, other times not at all. She tries to raise her girls honest, they way they had. Addie hoped she was doing it right.

"Fallon, it is." Addie prayed this was a phase, with four dollies she let it go. Thankfully, it only lasted one summer. That was the first summer without her mother. Summers' became tradition, six treasured weeks at the Cove. The first summer, Georgia was still her child. The little girl in a big hurry to grow, she missed out, the details. She never lived in the moment, always dreaming ahead. Addie tried to explain; Georgia didn't listen. Addie missed Harry, even the heated arguments. She was so fucking pissed off. How could she go on, without her? She had Caden, her harem of honey and daddy a while longer. Who would tell her the truth when she got it wrong? When she was fucking up? She'd have to figure it out. No one could replace her. Who would take the reins scared the crap out of her. What if she did a heinous job with them. Fuck cancer. Fucking cancer ripped her family apart. She had to go on, her babies were counting on her.

Zack turned away from his daughter, staring out at the ocean, lost at sea. He smiled. Pretty knew, he'd always known. Harry was magic. "Daddy, stop. I see you."

Zack turned to his daughter, raised his Corona to the sky. Adelaide wiped ketchup off Z-Z's chin. They burst out laughing, tears rolled down their cheeks. The harder they tried, the rowdier they got. The girls stood to clear the table, barely noticing. Z-Z hugged her pop pop, exhausted from a full day of sand, sea and fun. She yawned and yanked Trudy by the arm. Dutifully, Trudy followed. Harry's namesake, she was the easiest. Maybe Harry decided her daughter needed one child that didn't make a ruckus. Gertrude was bee's honey, delightful, most polite. Caden's girl, she curled in his lap on the couch, falling asleep, nuzzled in his arms. Her sisters didn't mind, they watched TV, pestered each other. Caden carried Trudy upstairs, into the sunflower bedroom she shared with Zelda, to tuck her in. To Trudy and daddy bedtime was precious; Adelaide adored her husband. Watching him with his daughters, made her heart full.

Trudy and Z-Z sang, swinging their little arms high, all the way to the porch. It's true, twins have their own language, mannerisms, invisible mirrors. She wondered when it would happen, that they'd split apart. She prayed not soon, she wanted them to stay together, forever.

"I'll be up. Brush your teeth, fishies." Adelaide swung one leg around the bench, walked to her dad and gave him a bear hug. She began the trek to the house, garbage bag in tow, mentally prepping for bedtime rituals. Not before she stopped, to turn back. Sneak a peek at her daddy, blow him a kiss. His back to her, facing the ocean deep in thought. Missing Harry. Adelaide understood this by his posture, the way his jaw clenched, how he held the beer bottle with two hands. She knew where he'd gone, to her. She frowned, blew him a kiss anyway. Thanks mom, we needed a good laugh. Stop putting ideas in their peanut brains. Her name is *Maxine*, not Fallon. So pretentious, where'd you come up with that? Busting my balls, I hear you mother.

Addie stressed over the twins, checked on them two or three times a night. She couldn't help herself; they were so tiny. She was afraid to pick them up when they were newborns. Terrified she'd hurt them, sobbed when she brought them home. That first month, Addie refused to leave the den, constantly yelling at Georgia and Max to be careful. Caden tried reasoning, nothing worked. Zelda and Trudy were perfect, healthy. Harrison barged in with a double stroller and babysitter for Max and Georgia.

"You have twenty minutes, missy. We're going out with the twins. You look like shit." Adelaide started to cry.

"Cut the theatrics or I'll take them without you." Addie jumped off the couch, knowing her mother meant business. She hurried to her bedroom, threw on jeans, clean t-shirt and cardigan. Harrison knew the snide remark would get Addie off the couch.

"Comb the mop, brush your teeth. Chop-chop." Adelaide was never so grateful to see her mother. That was a great day. Harry did that, she could take your worse days and throw them in your face. Make you face your fears, move on. Addie never worried about Zelda and Gertrude again, went about her days. Z-Z was safe, content in the playpen with Trudy attached to her breast. And, vice-versa. Maxine amused herself outside the playpen playing, coloring, singing to them. She was never far from her mama's reach.

Georgia was a different story. She was quiet. Painfully quiet. Harrison had left Georgia in the den. Addie had a first class migraine, her mother propped Georgia on the couch with pillows, her blanket and Disney DVD. Harrison would never say it, Georgia got the bum rap. Being the oldest, she got shuffled around. She was up to no good, Addie could tell from her silence. Little shit. She set Trudy in the pen next to Z-Z, fast asleep. Trudy snuggled close to her sister, angels, her miracle easy babies. Georgia had splattered multi-color paint on the white wall, in every shade imaginable. Jackson Pollack gone mad. Addie looked at her daughter, sorbet of rainbow color drenched in paint, she was stunning. Made her smile, despite the pounding head.

"Bathtub young lady, clothes and all. Do NOT touch the faucets. I'm serious." Georgia stopped on the stairs, sticking out her tongue leaving tech-color footprints on each plank behind.

"Your father just sanded those." Addie checked on the twins, picked up Maxine and headed upstairs. "What'd she do now, do I have to come? It's not fair. She ruins everything, wait and see mama." Adelaide hated Max's predictions, they were usually right. The splattered paint imprint of tiny soles on the wooden stairs made a trail to the bathroom. Georgia's escapades frightened her sister. Max held tight to her mother's hand. She handed her naked daughter a garbage bag for the soiled clothes.

"But nana says, *free-damn of expression*."

"Georgia, I don't give two hoots what your grandmother says." Maxine claps.

"Shut up, weirdo. *I hate you*." Georgia splashes her sister perched on the stool, bored and annoyed.

"Can I go?" Addie nods, scrubbing Georgia's naked butt forcefully with a loofah.

"Ouch." Georgia scowls at her mother.

"Do not wake them, I mean it. Georgia leave Max be. No Play Station, TV, iPad, no gadgets two weeks. Your grandmother is in deep shit."

"Language!" Georgia and Max yell in unison.

"I can't wait to get the hell out of here. Freaks. I'm going to California. *I hate you all*." Georgia screams, storms off to her bedroom, towel wrapped around her burning head. The high priestess, naked, dripping body with clenched fists, slamming the door.

"Pajamas."

Adelaide scrubbed, watching the ice cream swirls disappear down the drain. She knew Georgia was a direct descendent of Harrison, same mannerisms, coloring, fearless, brash, mouthy attitude. It would get her in trouble, someday. Addie prayed for her girls, her husband and dad every night. For Georgia she prayed double, God would keep her alive. When her mom died, Georgia wouldn't leave Adclaide's side. She not only understood her mama's grief, she felt it. Sorrow and melancholy became part of her. Georgia begged her to let her go, stay with Zack. He needed her. Addie refused, until she couldn't stand it anymore. "But, mama you know I'm right. He's a doctor, what could happen? I'll be fine." Georgia was relentless, kept at it. She even wore Caden down.

"Fine, one month this summer, if you keep your grades up. Your sisters and I are coming."

"What?! NO way."

"Yes. Way. I'm flying out, getting you settled. I swear, if you even look at Maxine sideways, I'll fly you and your shitty attitude right back. Pops will report, every night. Play nice, help around the house. You want to be grown-up, one wrong move smarty-pants."

"Whatever. I swear you are the ugliest, meanest bitch." Addie slapped Georgia, across the face. Georgia stood immobilized, mouth wide open in shock. She pushed too far. She wasn't sure who looked more surprised, her or her mother. She never mouthed off again, once was plenty.

Adelaide flew all the girls to Cali to stay with her dad. She didn't mean to stay, a day turned into a week. She slept in her mother's room, with Max. She forgot how much she loved this house, mystic place full of memories. Harrison occupied every corner, it was healing to be home. The ocean mended her spirit, she spent lazy days on the beach with her daughters, enjoyed Zack's infamous cookouts. Addie even waxed her board, donned a wetsuit. The girls hooted and hollered, teasing their mama. Until they saw her catch a wave, they screamed and clapped. She couldn't leave, how could she go back to Maine when her broken heart was home. Caden didn't need an explanation, he understood by her tone.

"Stay, babe. It's a mend-cation. The house is too quiet, weird." Addie laughed. She knew her husband was walking around in boxers, sleeping late, drinking beer at noon and watching the History Channel, relishing peace and quiet. He was a marine biology professor now, summers off. She knew he was a diver first, missed the expeditions, thrill, the aquatic life. Caden gave it up when she got knocked-up with the twins. He didn't have to; Harry left her daughter a mega inheritance. Her films were cult classics, money kept pouring in. Harrison would've loved that. Caden was too proud, he wouldn't take a dime except the Maine house. They were babies when they met, he was no match for Adelaide's over-bearing, controlling mother. He agreed to the house, keep the Harry-in-law quiet.

Caden didn't want to miss a thing. Not one first tooth, haircut, word, smile, not one milestone with his angels. Caden was better than her; she wasn't ashamed to admit it. He was kind, calm, sweet, sexy, a kickass husband and father. Maybe they could work something out, she could bring the girls to the Cove next summer, he could plan an expedition. He would never admit, he missed the life, the dives, Alaska, killer whales, no one tugging his jeans. "Hold on, babe. Trudy wants to say something." Caden knew what she wanted, but played along. Not one milestone, would go missing.

Duct Tape

Sometimes X could not believe the shit that came out of her head, shocked her. Georgia could be mean, snake venom evil. Her own mother never would put up with the back talk, hand stinging her cheek before X knew what happened. Legs or no legs, she did not stand foul language, disrespect. X worried about that fire belly. She made a promise to Harrison, she'd keep her out of trouble. Georgia'd get there, there was no light without experimenting in the dark. X liked the fancy new keyboard, lit transparent blue at night, weighing nothing. She typed and typed, scarcely felt it. She'd seemed happier, lighter, Bossy commented. "Did you take care of her, Seven?"

"Yes." Bossy sponged bathed her quickly, careful she didn't catch cold.

"The letter explaining everything, six months. Did you open the account? Where's she going? What's first? Tell me everything. She's going to wait, right? *You* told her."

"God, we went over this yesterday. Yes, I sent the letter. Yes, opened the e-account. You are so annoying. She'll wait for the damn book. Might head west, see Redwoods, walk the Golden Gate. She promised to send the pre-stamped postcards. That's it, all I got. Shouldn't you be typing?"

"If you hurry, I'm frozen."

Bossy swats X's arm. "It's 85 degrees your highness, zip it." Bossy reaches under X's pits, swings her to the edge. "Arms." X lifts her arms, bossy pulls an XXL, long sleeve, men's cozy top over her head, tugging.

"Why so big, you look like a footballer," her mom asked once.

"Duh, *like hello*." X hid her body best she could

"Anything else?" Bossy would be back at 7:00 to help her to bed.

"Lock the door." X didn't like people barging in. Except the ones in her head; she dug them. She wished her world was just like Harry's. Wishing didn't help, waste of headspace. The story is mapped out, scenarios set. Damn Georgia is taking her sweet time, holding her hostage. She'd show her, move it along Georgia Pine.

The Progeny & Beat Down Leather Backpack

The second baggage claim doors opened, Georgia took a deep, cleansing breath. Sunny Cali in June, palm trees greeted her by name, she whipped off the woolen peacoat, got in the cab lane. She loosened her long locks, running her hands through the tangled mess. She felt the envious eyes, it wasn't the black orchid tattoo, her towering height, lithe, supple body or fuck-off attitude that accompanies the age. She'd be eighteen in 28 days. The flaming, enviable hair cascading down her back was the main attraction. She jumped in a cab, opened the backpack, dumpster diving for her cell. She meant to clean the mess.

"I'm here. Yup, 75 and sunny. No, I already told you. Goddamn, I'll call the second I see him, swear. Get a job or something, ma. So annoying, hanging up." She was always on her ass. Georgia couldn't wait to get away, far from that loony bin. Her sisters were whack jobs, and her mother. Ugh, uptight was being kind. She was here. Zack couldn't come to the airport, revoked license. Try living in Hollywood without a ride. Addie hired *Solange*, some Frenchie to run errands, laundry, take him to the doctor. She was a B- actress in France, always in the tabloids with some famous dude. She was a type, but that accent. What a waste, she was sweet to him. That was something. As soon as Georgia pulled off the highway onto the winding road down to the cottage, she sat up hugging the driver's headrest. She felt giddy like a child, knees trembling. She spotted him before they pulled in, sitting in his rocker all alone, blanket covering his knees. Silver hair freshly combed, he was sleeping, mouth open. He looked so fragile. He should've come back to Maine last summer, she told her mom. Stupid cunt, never listens. Pops wouldn't budge anyway. It must be 80, what gives with cashmere? Georgia slumped back in the torn, sticky leather seat, rubbing her dry eyes. She was dehydrated, exhausted; jet lag had set in. She tied her hair back, put on some lipstick, paid the driver, grabbed her duffle from the trunk quietly, and swung the tattered backpack over her shoulder. She tiptoed up the porch, trying not to wake him. He opened his eyes and saw her silhouette, smiling his Georgia smile.

"What took you so long, I've been waiting." Georgia got weepy, she knew he wasn't talking about her. "Pop, it's me. You need a shave. That dumbass Franc taking care of you?"

"Georgia Pine, 'bout time. My eyes play tricks, don't pick on Solange."

"Sure. Everything's cool, I'm here. It's going to be a great summer. I'm going to dump my stuff on the bed, want anything? Water? Tea?"

Zack looked up, and squeezed her hand tight. "Got everything I need, right here."

Georgia half-smiled, stupid Maxine and her premonitions. She pecked her grandfather's cheek, went to Harry's old room, threw her duffle on the chair. Lying on cozy, inviting embroidered quilt for a second, promptly passing out. It's dark when she finally wakes, disoriented. She hears her dead grandmother's voice, whispering in her ear. She speaks slowly, methodically.

Georgia Pine. Remember our talks. Be nice to your mother. She needs you, she won't ask. Your sisters, they're all you've got. You'll see, wear your hair down, loose and free. You don't have to act so goddamn stoic. Trust me, wasted a lot of years pretending." Georgia starts to cry, rocking back and forth. *"The*

Cove will be here. When you need refuge, the magic remains. The ocean is our conduit, the waves carry messages between us.

She sat up, afraid what might be lurking. "Don't be scared, go on." Georgia wanted to strangle her grandmother. Always poked and pushed.

"Fine." Georgia leaves the bedroom and looks for her grandfather. He's sitting at the kitchen table, set for two. Take-out containers sit on the counter top, barely touched fish sits on his plate. Relieved, she plops down in the chair, jug of water in hand. "Sorry, pops."

Zack shakes his head, "went ahead without you."

"No worries. I was zonked."

"I know, checked your pulse."

Georgia laughs, reheating a plate. "Did not. I'm starving."

"Did too, goose. Looked like a red cardinal wings spread, dreaming on fluffy white down."

"Whatever."

"What do you say we surf? That is, if you can get your butt out of bed before noon. Lazy bones."

"Please, bet I have to wake you." Georgia doesn't want to surf. She used to be first in the water, now she's more into boys and music. It's the others that love it, the entire family sans Max. Georgia hates the tight wetsuits, sharks, freezing water, pre-dawn mornings. Hell, if the old man was up for it, she would do anything for him. She wonders, when the precise, worst moment of her life would strike. She couldn't do a damn thing about it. She was powerless, except surf. That, she could do.

"Be right back. You alright?"

"Where you going in the dark?" As if Zack didn't know, to check her flowerbeds. Make sure he hadn't let them turn into slosh pits. They're glorious, an array of exotic colors, flora in various shapes and sizes. Who was she kidding? Harry would've killed him if he let them rot. He fed, watered and pulled the weeds year round. Zack had replanted the seed, Georgia toiled the earth all summer. Made him drive to the nursery fifty times, scouring the internet which were the perfect perennials for the climate. Georgia, unlike her grandmother, had a green thumb. She made him send her pictures. By the following summer, even Addie was amazed. "Your grandmother would be jealous. It's glorious." His plan worked, she arrived a precocious sixteen year old, bitchy, mouthy, know it all. She left, his precious grandchild, sobbing in the truck. Pretty's bubbly, prankster, funny darling was in there. He knew all along, had to peel back the layers to find bottled sunshine, hard work and salt of the earth. She was so much like Harry, it made him hurt.

"Looks good, pop. See you, bright and early." Georgia wrapped her arms around him, crimson cascades tickling his face. He adored this child, made the empty, silence bearable. Zack looked around the outdated kitchen, Harry's things in place, right where she left them. Adelaide wanted to renovate, modernize a bit. Only time Zack refused his daughter, stood his ground. He never moved back into their bedroom. Couldn't. Zack took in his surroundings, black and white kitchen table, scratched windowsill, miniscule holes in the wall from pushpin calendars, sticky notes. He didn't feel the tear until it reached his lip, moist and salty. Strange, he was a doctor who knew better. Pretty was over-due for a checkup. Didn't bother. They'd be fine without him. He'd been a lovesick patient far too long.

Ripple Effect

Georgia called her mama screaming, Addie couldn't make out one word. "Take a breath darling, what's wrong? Georgia, you're scaring me. What's happened …" In an instant, Addie's legs gave out. She collapsed to the bedroom floor. Caden lunged like a cougar, at her side in seconds. He touched her head, arms. Addie shoved him away.

"Are you hurt, the girls? Adelaide." She doesn't hear him through the howls. A vision plays over and over in her mind. She must have been seven or eight, couldn't remember the year. She was straddling a pastel, blue surfboard with a white wave on the open ocean. The sea was calm, there were no waves, only tiny ripples. The sun felt warm, must have been midday. She glanced to her side, there he was, nodding and smiling. Her daddy, and no one else's. The wrinkles wiped from his pretty face, hazel eyes dancing. Biceps bulging under the wetsuit, he was strong. It was their special place, his and hers. Mommy didn't like the water; she didn't come. Addie was secretly happy to have him all to herself. His lips moved, she couldn't make out the words. "Daddy, I can't hear you," Adelaide screamed in fetal position. He mouthed the words again, slowly and precisely.

"I love you, have to go." He nodded, their love wrapped in one sentence. He paddled off, in the opposite direction. She tried desperately to follow, keep up, her little legs and arms simply gave out. She could not catch him.

"Daddy, stop. Please," she sobbed. "Don't go, pretty please. I'm scared, don't paddle so far out," she screamed. Adelaide tried to sit up, control her shallow breath. She lay on the bedroom carpet, picking at fibers. She couldn't see him. He disappeared into a sea of blue nothing, froth and foam. The sun was blinding, obscuring her view. She glanced down at her board, it was long and burnt orange. That wasn't right, her hands and feet were no longer pint-size. She was an adult, tan, soaked golden waves hung loose. Adelaide sat up wiping snot, grabbed a pillow from the bed hugging it between her knees. She reached for Caden's hand, not realizing he'd been there with her all along.

"Daddy. Oh Christ, Georgia."

Caden dialed back his wracked daughter, rattling off instructions. "Call Harry's Jenny, then 911. You can do this, stop crying honey. I need you to breathe. The number is on the wall; Jenny knows what to do. She'll take care of everything. Check into a hotel or stay with her, whichever you want. Use the emergency credit card." He promised he'd call right back, needed to make flight arrangements, round up the girls. Phone his sisters; let them know. "Hold tight, Georgia. Daddy and Mommy are coming."

"Oh Addie," picking her up and gently setting her on the bed. She felt like a rag doll, entire body limp. They were barely twenty years old when they met, she was his gypsy girl, surfing queen, and goddess of the sea. He knew he was too young to settle down, he knew he loved her bigger than a missed adventure. She was it. His life with her, the girls felt like a permanent staycation. Zack had been fair, generous and kind. Showing up at Adelaide's parents doorstep with their knocked up daughter. He would've killed the bastard. Addie was six months along, Harry was furious. Caden was not her favorite person. Zack talked to Harry, cajoled, calmed her wild temper. He even rented the yacht, threw them the most beautiful wedding, such a great guy. Caden would miss him; he was secretly happy though. He caught the longing, faraway look in Zack's eyes when he thought no one was watching. He missed her. Zack taught Caden how to '*handle*' his mercurial woman.

"Step way back," he said. "Be patient. She'll get curious, come looking." Sure enough, he was right. Cade checked the clock on his phone, 4:00 a.m. If they hurried, they'd make the noon flight.

Dance Party Playlist

She didn't sleep, restless. Harry the nuisance, kept popping in and out of the dream state. Georgia told her to get lost. By six, she couldn't take it. She was starving, jet lagged and grumpy. She made coffee and toast. Surprise him, breakfast in bed. Ha, he'd never believe she was awake, ready to go. She used the bathroom, peed on the frozen toilet seat, washed her face. The tap was ice cold. He must have forgotten to set the thermostat last night. Georgia headed down the hall toward the kitchen, morning sun casting bizarre shadows. Odd, something was on the kitchen table. She thought she had cleared it. Georgia felt a gust of wind breeze past, her stomach cramped. Nice, grandma. The closer she went, the clammier she got. She checked his room, bed was made like it hadn't been slept in. Maybe he passed out on the sofa, he did that sometime. She peeked her head in the den, empty couch. Stood in the kitchen archway a good five minutes, working up the nerve to go in. Come on pussy, what are you waiting for? Georgia knew that's why Harry blew past. He sat right where she left him, in his chair, head on the table. He wasn't moving, maybe it was a heart attack. They could fix that.

"Grandpa?" Georgia whispered nudging him with a pencil. Nothing.

"Pops," she screamed. She avoided the table best she could, clinging to the countertops. Harrison was in tears watching the scene, unable to reach out. She whispered a lullaby, hoping she'd hear. Georgia wasn't listening, the kitchen was closing in on her. She went fuzzy, everything turned black.

"THIS IS NOT HAPPENING, GODDAMN YOU. WE'RE SUPPOSED TO GO SURFING." Georgia screamed, and ran to the screen porch. She sat in *his* rocker in her nightshirt, pulling her knees into her chest, screaming in pain. Her stomach was killing her, she felt like she might hurl. Stop it, think. Okay. She needed her cell fuck, it was in *there*. She'd go around back. Georgia grabbed the plaid blanket from the closet and her backpack. The cell and charger were buried inside. All the while, Harrison never left. She was sobbing as they rocked. Reliving earth memories. Sophia, Katia, Pretty. She forgot how much it hurt to be alive. She missed it still, not the hurt, the juicy bits. Delirious to have him back, the mother in Harry shattered for Adelaide, his dollies, Georgia Pine and all the love that got left behind. All this time, Harry hadn't thought about Zack. The life he made without her, the hearts that would be broken. He was waiting down by the beach, her virile, strong, sexy, Dr. Pretty beckoning. She didn't need to look; she felt the familiar, loving embrace. Harrison Gertrude felt safest in his arms. She could hardly contain herself; yet she couldn't leave. Not yet. Poor baby was a mess. Oh Georgia, don't. You have so much life in front of you, so many adventures, so much love. She'd wait for their daughter to arrive, one last kiss. When she went to him, that was it. They belonged to the ether, no more hovering. No more Cove visits, no more family, colors, sunsets, no Himalayan pink seas, no lingering, no touch, no empty. They couldn't cross back. Zack didn't know, she made the decision for both. A sacred pact between God and a panic stricken, bald, desperate, dying woman. One thousand moon cycles, she was free to come and go, visit the Cove. One thousand moon cycles was all she asked, what she got. It wasn't enough. It would be too soon for him to digest. Harry didn't regret it. All roads lead back to Zack.

Froth and Foam

Georgia did not dare move from that porch. She watched Jenny, Harrison's longtime assistant, pace. Her Bluetooth blinking from her ear, doodling, jotting down notes. The over efficient Jenny loved Harry; despite the bad behavior, she meant well. Zack, she adored him. He made her job easier, Harry softened. Jenny never had to *work* again, Harrison left her a generous inheritance with a sticky note, "for pain and suffering." The ambulance pulled up, no sirens. Guess when you're dead, there are no bells and whistles. Damn, he deserved fireworks. Georgia would make sure he got them. The EMT's were laughing and gossiping. As if this was some ordinary day. "SHUT IT," Georgia barked. Jenny came flying out, "what's going on?" Georgia motioned toward the truck, staring the bald dude down, while fat belly opened the back. His eyes fixed ahead, scared of the crazy chick on the porch, pulling out the gurney. She couldn't do this, Georgia bolted to the beach. She sat in the wet sand, coarse grains scratching her butt. She didn't care, the pain felt good. Zack was beside her, sitting Indian style, elbows perched on his knees, hands under his chin. Anyone but her, this was not good. He desperately wanted to wipe her face with his sleeve, comfort her. His precocious funny face, fire and ice, electric granddaughter. Harry was there too; Zack couldn't see her yet. It takes time to grasp the concept. Not being alive walking the earth, accept death. Georgia's sadness barreled over them, her pain pulsating the vein on her forehead. A dark, somber teenager, she might not bounce back. She wasn't fun. She wasn't dense, she knew. He lied, told her she was funny. She believed him, stupid fuck. She relived the morning, questioning every step. Why did she go to bed, why didn't she wait for him? Maybe she could have gotten to him in time. She retraced her steps. She couldn't know; death is predestined. The precise day, hour, minute, second, where and how, inscribed in utero. She would get answers, farther down the road. The only emotion she felt was pain. Like nothing she'd experienced, a black sinkhole. It was nightfall, Georgia turned towards the house. The lights were on, a warm, translucent yellow glow drifted through the rooms. Candlelight.

At the top of the hill, she saw her. The distant shadow, erect. She stood stoic, watching. The long, envious curls air born, arms crossed, fringe shawl covering her body. Georgia started to bawl, too drained to move, she watched her mother descend each step in the pitch dark, no flashlight necessary. This was her world, Adelaide knew every rock, nook, pebble on the way down. The cement steps, secret burial nooks held hidden notes, desires, fears, childhood dreams, first kiss, true loves, babies, her father and mother's imprints. Music drifted from the house, melodies accompanied days spent at her beach. She wasn't sure exactly, how she'd make it down those rocks without him. Embrace her with his strong, tan, loving arms. Her daddy was always there, waiting. She saw her firstborn, lying alone in the dark, curled up on wet, angry sand, and she knew. This wasn't about her, or him. He'd given her all his love. It was about being a mother to the broken child who needed her. Adelaide said nothing, she lay down next to her crimson beauty, covering her with Harry's cashmere shawl. Georgia was shivering; Addie did not move, did not dare. She waited, unsure who was grieving more. Zack had so much love, no one drew the short stick.

"Mommy?" Addie's tears hitting the sand. She didn't speak, terrified to say the wrong thing. "Was it me?" Adelaide could barely stand it, "don't be silly. You were his favorite, don't tell your sisters."

"Can we throw a party, no sappy funeral? He wouldn't want that. Get on the boards, paddle him out."

"It's late, you're freezing. Your sisters and dad are waiting." Georgia sat up, rubbed her head, looked at her mother and stood, offering her hand. Adelaide's fragile heart melted, she smiled and grabbed her daughter's wrist. Georgia became a woman that summer, by default. Adelaide was incredibly proud, Harry was right. The good men in her life were instrumental. They made their way to the stairs, sky covered in steel bright stars, illuminating the rocks. Addie glanced back at the midnight blue ocean, the vast landscape, half expecting to see him standing there, watching mother and daughter, pleased grin, satisfied nod. She didn't see him, yet she knew he was there. She squeezed Georgia's hand, "I think he would love a party."

"Mom? He loved you best." Adelaide wrapped her arms around her sullen, difficult daughter. Georgia didn't flinch, she let her mother hold her. He loved *Harry* best, Addie thought. She'd settle for second. She couldn't compete with her mother. The funeral wasn't a funeral at all. Georgia made a list of items for Jenny to pick up. Checkered picnic tablecloth, mason jars, tea lights, indigo, bright orange, turquoise, lemon colored sky lanterns, hotdogs, hamburgers, corn, green beans, sweet tea, lemonade and one thousand floatable ECO candles. 80's pop music played from the ancient boom box. Caden manned the grill. She and her sisters laughed, told stories about him, the Cove, the awful fish he cooked they never ate. Pops throwing them into the ocean, teaching them to swim, snorkel, read, ride bikes, break up fights, teach them to drive. He was so proud, made sure they had alone time. He turned into a vigilante when the surfer dudes came around. His laugh was contagious; he tickled his dolls until they screamed for mercy. He was rigid when it came to their safety, drowning them with his love.

Maxine was moping, way quieter and weirder than usual. Georgia stormed over annoyed, tapped her shoulder and scooted her butt down the bench. "Spill."

"They're gone." Maxine started to sob. Georgia placated her, she was allowed to feel sad. It gets dangerous to let Maxine wallow too long.

"Zip it."

"Pretend happy face, for mom. Put on your wetsuit, we are *all* going. Move it, that means you." Maxine stared at Georgia with hate, bulging ice eyes, challenging her. Georgia felt icky all over; she gave Max a shove. "*Not now.*"

"They're gone. Like, forever. You think you're so smart, fucking cunt." Maxine bolted for the porch, bloodstain tears streaming down her alabaster cheeks. Georgia never got her, until now. There would be no more night whisperers, shadows, shivers, starfish wishes, messages in code. Maxine was right; they were gone.

"Wetsuits, people." Jenny knew that was her cue to get the candles lit and into the water. She hired a few locals to help. They refused to get paid; everyone loved Zack. He was a fixture at the Cove. When someone was hurt, sick, he was on call. Never charged a dime, happy to help. Zack and Harry waited for them on the beach, side by side. Take it in Pretty; we won't be back. What a strange sight, to watch the folks he loved, his people descend the stairs, wetsuits on and surfboards in hand. It would be kinda' hilarious, if it wasn't so damn sad. He didn't feel blue, he felt proud. The life he and Harry had, was magnificent. They created all this. Adelaide carried the cardboard box guardedly, tucked under her arm. She was weepy, not because she was sad, because the moment was historical, perfectly executed. The water was warm, surfers moved down the coast out of respect. Everyone paddled out, even Maxine. Floating candles illuminated the sea, his family formed a circle on their boards. Jenny sent twenty sky lanterns in clementine, indigo, lemon, emerald and bright, happy colors floating to the heavens. Adelaide gasped at the sky, glanced at Georgia's crinkled face. Georgia felt her mother's eye, gave her a half-smile, no words necessary. She nodded. Adelaide smiled through tears, opened the lid and set Pretty free. He was her first love, teacher, protector, her first everything, true love. He showered her with so much kindness, compassion, patience, confidence and adventure. As fathers go, she could not dream another. She took in the ocean, intimate circle of love, studying each face carefully, every teardrop. She was grateful for her little humans, almost grown, her sexy, ragged, sensitive, blond mop top, loyal husband. Her daddy was the sparkler that lit her life, made all things possible. He was the centrifuge, balancing force, her daughters' roadmap to life, summers at the beach, memories that shine and disappear behind the clouds. And more. The amazing and tragic, Addie couldn't wait to see his smiling face again. He taught her she was enough. Harrison Gertrude may have been the driving force, her daddy was the roads, potholes, mountains, gravel and seas they travelled upon.

"See you later, daddy." She was sure her precocious mother was celebrating, dancing freestyle. Addie's goose bumps ran up and down her tight, rubber-clad arms. He was saying good-bye, and thank you. Sorry, he had to go. He'd stay wrapped, tangled and sealed inside her beautiful, beating heart. Not good-bye golden ringlet girl, *you* have my heart. Harry was anxiously waiting, to be reunited with her one and only. Adelaide lost in too many memories, saw dots on land, painted surfboards tossed about. The candles dimmed, the beach looked like a scene out of a film noir, her mother the shining star. Spirit shadows dancing, violet umber evening summer. She wet her face with salt water trying to wash the tears away. "I have to go take care of our dollies. I'll miss this, daddy. Our special time, just me and you." Addie closed her eyes, took a deep, cleansing breath and began to paddle, one stroke at a time.

Batten the Hatches

It was time. Three weeks at the Cove. Swimming, laughing, crying, overeating, doing the things normal people do when they lose someone. Sophia wanted to come out, Katia too. Addie told them not to bother. They were her mother's best friends, confidantes. Since she died, they visited Adelaide in Maine three, four times a year. They were Zack's friends, too. Sophia was in perfect health, she'd live to be one hundred. There was no point to the long trek, besides Adelaide wanted to be alone with her husband and daughters. Sophia understood. Katia was well, Katia. Addie never quite understood their friendship, spanning decades and continents between them. They were so different, her mother and Katia, oil and water. Katia infuriated Harrison, pushed her limits. Harry pushed right back. She called, hysterical when Harry died. She'd never forget that feeling, pain shot straight through the wireless sky. Heavy shit, Katia wanted to keep Harry strong, make her fight. Did she say the wrong thing, Addie wondered? Katia had three Eco hotels, Quinn, her daughter, was single and eight months pregnant. Adelaide told her not to come. Katia got weepy, old age. She loved Zack, he was the best thing about Harrison. Smoothed the jagged edges.

Adelaide went to the bedroom, dropped on her mother's bed. The linens were new, smelled like jasmine. Jenny had cut garden-fresh flowers from the garden, the house smelled like a tropical forest, exotic and enticing. Caden took the girls hiking, they'd be back before dinner. Peace and calm, Caden would pick something up. He knew Addie was exhausted, hadn't had a second to grieve. Georgia stayed behind. She was outside tending her flowerbeds, pulling weeds. She sat immobile for hours, staring blankly at the dirt. She was having a rough time, Zack's death hit her hard. When Harry died, Georgia took her place. Zack found refuge in her. Addie didn't mind. She used to take Georgia for ice cream, special time. Zack did the exact same when she visited. Sitting on a bench one afternoon, enjoying the Cali sun, a brown and white fluff puppy came bouncing over, snatched her twist cone. Georgia giggled and laughed so hard tears fell on her face, pops started laughing and giggling with her. That was the first time she remembered not seeing the sadness on his face. He was happy, wiping her chin and kissing her cheek. Georgia never told anyone it was *their* moment, his and hers. He laughed a lot after that day. She wondered, as she moved the dirt if she would ever laugh again, sans the hurt.

Crystalline Delicious

Seven was shocked when she opened the mailbox, a letter addressed to *her*.

X wrote, explaining in detail what she planned. Seven was surprised, walked around with her head buried in her books. She wouldn't tell him. He'd get suspicious, the bank account, secrecy, mysterious postcards. Besides, it was meant for her. He hated handouts, he'd never approve. Probably lock her in the barn with the stench. Nah, he'd never do that. He was a hypocrite, running around New York, making her mom fall for him, bringing her here, to the Bayou. Pretending everything was fine, a big, fat falsifier. She could hear him at the dinner table.

"Opal Jett, you know better. Don't expect no favors. What could some fancy author want with the likes of you? Famous? Horseshit." It was best not to tell, she hated keeping stuff. She'd get a job in New Orleans, he couldn't object. Better start saving. She was eighteen, legal. Wonder what her mother would think; she didn't know. She only knew the stories he told her, when she could get him to talk. Which was hardly ever. But one night, awoken from a nightmare crying out for her mother, her father talked. Told her a tale about when they first moved here.

Elizabeth took 'the test,' hid it in her panty drawer. He'd turn eggplant before he'd snoop through her underwear drawer. She knew without asking. He'd wanted a boy. Boys were no trouble, bucket of fried chicken, matchbox cars, sports kept 'em quiet. Liz knew the risks, exactly the same, boy or girl. 50/50 shot the child would carry the gene. She thought about not telling him, making some excuse to go to the city. New Orleans was an hour away, she could go early, be back before supper. She wished her own mother were here. She couldn't hide the tremors much longer, dropped dishes, keys left in the car, donating clothes with buttons, zippers were easier. It was happening, she was going to die. Huntington's was going to kill her.

She couldn't leave, she pinky swore. This baby might beat the statistics, she prayed long into the night. When she awoke, she knew he'd be up and gone. Farm life was not for sissies, and her husband was a tough, hardworking, God-fearing man. Lizzie fell for her young Adonis, literally into his arms. The awkward, shy, blond jock grew into a fine, decent man. He was worth it, deserved a happy life with a healthy wife and child. She decided as she dove under the bed in search of her slippers, half of happy was better than none.

She dressed, went downstairs to the antiquated, 1950's kitchen. The dime store clock on the wall read half past 7:00. She poured a cup of coffee from the kettle on the cast iron stove and sat on the porch. The haze lifted from the fields, yellow drops of sun glistened over the miles and miles of wet dew. He was far from her, riding his fancy, new toy. The John Deere tractor looked empty and forlorn, tilling the earth. He couldn't hear Liz, the cab stereo system blasting Guthrie. She waved anyway, for the hell of it. She'd tell him tonight, over dinner. Something in the lawn kept throwing sunbeams in her eyes, blinding her. A rock, she bet. So annoying, curious she walked to the shiny object. It wasn't a rock at all, but an *Opal*. She checked Wiki on her phone, browsed some images and found the exact Opal, matching the one in her trembling hand. *'Opal amongst quartz crystals flashes fire, gold and emerald.'*

The Louisiana Opal Mine had been shut down for years. Liz heard the town gossip, only one precious gem was found. Seems they missed one, unless it came from Australia. The poised, confident, well-mannered Lizzie was back. "Well baby *Opal*, it's very nice to meet you. Subtle, aren't ya?" Liz stroked her belly, content.

"I'm your mommy. Don't worry; I've got this. What do you say we head into town? I feel a chocolate cake craving coming on." She remembered the intoxicating, celebratory smell saturating her childhood kitchen, her mother swatting her butt with a spatula, whenever she tried to lick the beaters. Liz looked at her batting her lashes, her mom caved every time, handing over the gooey covered beaters.

She was sorry, so very sorry she'd run away without a proper goodbye. Her mother didn't deserve that. Liz only understood this minute, the heart-wrenching decision her mama had made. Abortion was never an option. Liz was still a child, how could she grasp the weight? Until, this. Opal. Her mother must have gone through the same wracking emotions, weighing them on her baker's scale. The same ones she was feeling. Cake batter made from scratch requires patience, love, the freshest ingredients and perfect timing. Her mother never watched the clock, she had baker's intuition, precision, instinct, tradition, trial, error and heart. Liz's mind was not yet on board with her decision; Opal already owned her heart. Head vs. heart, never you mind. Heart takes the long shot, wins. As she turned the sparkling, rough rock over and over in her hand, the shimmering facets made polka dots dance on her arm. Her mom would have loved that rock. Liz understood her mother's annoying prim, proper, pretty demeanor. She knew ugly might catch her someday. Elizabeth felt melancholy; her mom would never bake a cake for her granddaughter, rock her and sing lullabies. She regretted so many things about being eighteen, selfish, stubborn, foolish and naïve. Thought she had life figured out, realizing now she knew absolutely nothing.

Elizabeth was born with a fifty-fifty shot, she prayed bumping into Adonis upped them. He was her personal gem, rock steady and solid like quartz. If *she* had to die, she would leave him something so irresistible, delectable and rich, inviting. Better than chocolate cake.

Breakers

Adelaide roamed the halls of the cottage, grateful for the silence. Caden had taken the girls for the afternoon, except Georgia. Trudy and Z-Z couldn't wait, track suits, hiking boots, they were outside near the tree stretching, talking gibberish back and forth. Zelda was loosening her calves, while Trudy pushed them deep into her butt. "OW, quit it," swatting Zelda in the arm. Z-Z stormed off and sat on the picnic bench, pouting. Gertrude stuck her tongue out, they could never stay mad for long. Gertrude was getting boobs, turning into quite the pretty tween; her sister was jealous. She needed a little time to catch up. Z-Z was the late bloomer. "I hope we see a mountain lion, or rattlesnake. That would that be wicked," Zelda replied with fervor, tiff already forgotten.

"Duh, like you'll be dead before you see it." Trudy rolled her eyes, the EMO, exasperated teenager. "Dad has a gun, stupid."

"It's not a gun, it's a Taser. Won't do him much good when the lion bites his head off." Z-Z drops to the ground, playing dead. Spontaneous squeals, rolling around in the grass erupts, like little girls do. Addie watched from the kitchen window, her precious Gemini twins. This would be gone soon, the sweet, irreplaceable innocence. By next summer they'd be fighting over the same boy, slamming doors, mean, moody devils would appear. Powerless, she'd been through it with their sisters. Georgia challenged her, testing her will. Without her father and the Cove, she might have lost her. She was headed for real trouble. Drugs cost less than a pack of smokes, and there's a full-blown, epidemic in suburbia. What happened to keggers and smoking weed?

Caden pulled in with enough supplies for a week in the wild. Addie grinned remembering Seattle, Mount Rainier, cold, relentless rain, stuck in the flimsy, orange pop-up for days. They barely noticed, twenty and madly in love. Caden promised her a surfing trip, Addie missed the ocean, the breakers. Georgia was conceived on top of that mountain. She did not know then that her life was about to start. So high in the clouds, storms raging, close to the heavens, she knew. Bliss, joy, desire, she dare not move, afraid to jinx it. Georgia Pine, her grandmother affectionately called her. Her firstborn, nature baby made close to the earth, atop needles of pine.

Georgia didn't feel like hiking, dealing with her sisters. Addie told her to stay, help clean out Zack's things. Addie didn't tell her about the envelope. She had turned eighteen last week without much fuss. Everyone was sad and Georgia refused a *stupid, kiddy party.* Adelaide didn't force it, the sadness on her face matched how she felt. She wanted to comfort her child; Georgia was not big on hugs. She cringed, pushed her away. The letter she hoped, might help. Addie went to her mother's bedroom, opened the top drawer. There they were, after two decades, sealed, faded envelopes inside a plain, brown box. Addie brought the box to her nose eyes closed, inhaling, hoping for a trace of her mother. Nothing. She took a cleansing breath fighting tears, tearing the flap. Addie sat on the bed, spreading out four white business envelopes. Georgia, Maxine, Zelda and Gertrude. Wiping her foggy eyes she saw two more. She was confused. Wait, six. "I don't get it," she blurted aloud. Turning over the envelopes, she saw Sophia's, the girls and another one addressed to her in Zack's handwriting. It threw her. She scooted back on the bed propping the pillows. Holding the envelope to the window, afternoon sunlight, it looked like a key. Addie tore open the envelope, a jagged, odd-shaped, copper rusted key fell out. She picked it up, turning it over, running the grooves against her finger. She had doubles to the house, car; she was miffed she couldn't place it. Okay daddy, I'm stumped. What the hell is this? Addie set the key on the nightstand, and began to read. The paper was crisp, white, and hadn't had time to fade like the others.

To Adelaide,

My golden ringlet, funny fish, seashine, sunshine girl and breaker of my heart. If you are reading this, I'm sorry. I never meant to leave. Thank you, for sharing your beautiful angels. I counted down the winter months until summer and your arrival. When the Cove was filled with life, and tiny feet could be heard prancing down the halls. Watching your girls grow into lovely, young women has been my greatest gift. They bring me so much joy. I could write a book to express what you've meant to me, but there isn't enough paper. I am so proud. The key? Gotcha. Smarty pants. It's a rusty, worn key I found washed up on shore. Maybe it was the lost key to buried treasure. Pirates, gold, riches, rubles and sunken jewels miles beneath your beloved ocean. That key? Unlocked all the treasures I've known. Opened your mother's heart. That key? Unbolted the door so I could find you the day you were born. That key? Belongs to you now. Bring it on every adventure, joyous occasions and sad ones, too. So your mother and I find the door unlocked. You, Adelaide, are the keeper of the key. Everything I have, everything I own is yours. Ask Georgia to look after the Cove. She'll need something to tend to, to mend. See you later. Everything is going to be fine. Better than fine, wait for the break and paddle hard. I'll be beside you, enjoying the gnarly ride.

Love, Daddy

Gone Fishing

Adelaide placed the letter on the nightstand, slid beneath the comforting covers, key tight in her fist. She had a much needed, ugly cry. She'd been so busy, preoccupied with Zack's sisters, Katia and Sophia, Caden, the girls, endless phone calls. Jenny, sympathy cards, catering, senseless, morose death details, she didn't take a second for herself. To breathe, to stop, to process. Today was the first day of quiet since he'd gone. The dense twilight mist threatened violent, summer storms from the heavens; lightning, thunder and water pellets loomed. When she was a child, it wasn't Zack who could stop her fear and wails, it was her mother. Addie was petrified of thunderstorms as a kid, but only in summertime. It didn't make sense why the sky would be so angry. Harrison appeared at the doorway, watching her daughter toss and turn, matted hair, pillow soaked in tears. Not gushy and mush like her father, she didn't rush to the bed. She moved gracefully like a jaguar with a kill purpose. "What exactly are you afraid of, Adelaide? Remember every single detail." This was not the first time Harry had been awakened by her daughter's night terrors. She was making progress, less scared. Adelaide's tiny body stopped tossing; she had to think hard, concentrate on the rain hitting the roof. That was first. Harry listened intently, lovingly. She gave her a practical explanation for each fear. It took restraint not to go to Addie, rock her. Adelaide needed to learn to soothe herself. She remembered her mother's voice, the calming steps. Harry knew in her heart that was the best way to help.

Adelaide began processing the last weeks, breaking it down in segments, using the invaluable tools her mother taught her. She hadn't realized how many storms she had relied on those lessons. Labor, marriage, twins, worry, little humans, broken bones, peculiar Max, teen hormones, fights, Georgia, waterworks, doors slamming, death, grief. Her daddy was kind, loving, fun, athletic, affectionate, entertaining marshmallow, the buffer between her mom and herself.

When Harry died, she still had him. Zack was her constant, storm-free confidant. Now that they were both gone, who would balance the scales. She tried not to let the panic consume her, memories boiling over, pulling her under. The tears kept flowing, powerless to stop the mad, raging waters. Adelaide never realized when she mourned the loss of her father, she would mourn the loss of her mother all over again, and the moments of a magical life lived with mommy and daddy. Her childhood family had always been a constant in her life. She would never have them again. That kind of pain, sorrow, she could not rationalize, understand, step by step. She was the frightened child in the midst of a thunderstorm without shelter. Steps, there are no steps to rationalize death and love.

Adelaide let go, cocooned in a white cloud of down comfort. She slumbered, dreaming of plaid picnic blankets, baskets, melons, oranges, baguettes, brie, green olives and sweet tea. The citrine sunrays' shadow danced across the waves. The dream a memory. Her mother's strong, lean arms sending her soaring above the ocean. Free, unafraid, Adelaide saw her daddy waving on shore, peeling a Clementine.

Brooding, Georgia was bored and hungry. Daylight almost gone, she gathered her garden tools, rubbed the dirt from her hands and used the outdoor hose to rinse off. Slipping off her green, rubber boots she snuck in through the back. The house was dark; she began to sweat, scouring from room to room in frantic search for her mother. When she arrived outside the door to Harry's room, Georgia relaxed. She knew before she peeked, that her mom was there. One lock of long golden hair exposed was all she needed. She was fine. Georgia closed the door carefully, gently without a sound. The brats would be back, she'd keep them away.

The summer Georgia turned eighteen, her sheltered world collapsed. She took refuge in her spade and shovel. The gardens overflowed, magnificent exotic beds with no more space to grow. It was time for some serious pruning, make room for them to thrive and blossom. She had made a decision. Georgia wasn't going back to Maine. She wouldn't leave the Cove no matter what. It was high time to figure stuff out. Who the hell was she, what did she want? What were her dreams, not pop's. Not even her mom or dad's. She was suffocating without purpose; it was out there. Georgia would find it, life on her own. She could use Harrison's fame; agents had been hounding her mother for years. Easy was hers for the taking, fame, money, power, zero talent required. She hated the culture, the vapid world of sex tapes, greed, ego and bam. Instant celebrity. She watched her grandmother's films, cult classics. Harry was the real deal, raw, dark emotion. She got out before she became the pitiful stereotype, plastic old lady, tabloid fodder. Pops saved her, hell they saved each other. Georgia was a child when she died. Harrison's touch was electric. A day with her grandmother stuck long after she was gone. Her memory, infectious spirit, flowerbeds, ethereality, honest beauty, sharp tongue, lives and thrives in sacred corners at the Cove. The past embedded when you're lucky enough to know all consuming love. There was nothing trivial about Harrison; her direct descendants continue her legacy. That's what families do, families made from pure, tight together love. Georgia wanted to make her proud, might take time. She was making the first step, severing the lines. Scared, yet determined.

She wasn't going to college, damn straight. Four years imprisoned with spoiled, self-indulgent, Ivy League brats. No way, the wonder twins would make her annoying parents braggers and camera hogs. Zelda was taking college courses in high school. Gertrude had a soccer scholarship waiting. The effervescent, bubbly personalities were not an act. Seriously. She'd had enough happy, never needed her own. Miserable, Christ maybe it was true. Georgia was happy, not punch drunk stupid. She worried about Max. Georgia shut the mean kids down. They were terrified. Nobody touched *her* sister, no one except her. Georgia teased, taunted Max since forever. She tried to toughen her up. Maxine stayed kind, good. Too soft, too sensitive for the harsh cruel world she would never fit in. Georgia secretly wished she was a smidgen like Max; forgiving, non-judgmental, not a stink of vanity. Maybe someday she'd tell her. Who was she kidding; she would miss them. Her nutso family loved her, accepted the mercurial moods, faults and fiery temper. Some days she wished she had a fishing line drilled inside her mouth to wind back the insides that spilled out. Georgia spent her days apologizing and reeling it back. Teen angst, emo, that's who young girls are. She wasn't a teenager anymore. Death guts the growing process, hurtles you out of your element, thrashing, flapping and gasping for air. Losing your first love changes *every*thing. Georgia prays the fishhook and nylon tugging at her heart loosens. That it does not sever the Marianas Trench connection. She misses him; he is barely gone. Her grandfather would say, "I love you deep, like the Marianas Trench." Big words made her giggle; she was a little girl. She laughed a lot when she was with him. She understood the big words now, what they truly meant. They made the not so grown up Georgia cry.

Sorbet Splatter

Adelaide was taking a head count, checking the girls' rooms, beds made, bags packed. Caden climbed in bed late, not wanting to disturb the sleeping, sea goddess. It didn't feel like two decades. She was barely twenty when they met. Dumb luck, and timing. Some grunge band was playing at the Crocodile, Nirvana. A rock revolution was happening in Seattle, melodic sound spilled from every dorm. He'd catch the next show. Save the orca whales expedition, too good to miss. Grabbed his gear, ran to the pier, jumped aboard minutes before the ship left dock. Caden spotted his buddy's neon, orange parka at the bow, couldn't miss it. No rain, low swells, sun shining, textbook weather conditions for a pod sighting. Cade playfully nudged his friend, patting him on the back. He smirked, unzipped his backpack in search of his Nikon, brushing the blond curls from his face. He saw her, holding the rail, eyeing the ocean. Her towering silhouette, long, wavy, flaxen locks blowing free, gray raingear and beat-up, leather Birkenstocks. Her toes, painted neon green. He closed his eyes, recording the ethereal vision he'd just seen. Whales, what whales. She was the most beautiful creature in the Northern Hemisphere. Nothing had changed, the passion he first felt when she spun around. Their eyes met, she nodded, smiling. Two seconds, his trajectory was forever changed. Addie became his best friend, sea buddy, animal activist, adventure junkie, and lover. Twenty-three was way too young to fall deeply and madly in love. He didn't care, Adelaide was magnetic, her pure beauty and generous spirit, infectious. She was his confidante, challenger, mother of his babes. He was in awe of her, still. Zack was her anchor, buffer and safety net, he'd been fine with that. Zack was steady ground for them both. Cade heard Addie scurrying from room to room, barking orders, closing the house, he wanted to dive under the covers. If Zack were here, he'd slow her down. Caden kicked his feet out from under the duvet, reached for his jeans and t-shirt, went in search of his grief-stricken wife. "Don't remind her who she is, *show* her." Zack's advice when shit got crazy. Addie sat at the kitchen table, black coffee, two sugars, steaming hot, to-do list, gnawed pencil, twirling a strand of hair. Oh shit, the twirl so not good. Caden bent down, kissed her neck, peeking at the long list, only a third crossed off. He reached for her hand and cautiously removed the pencil. "Babe, I got this. Let's stay a few more days. Surf, sun, beach, winter's long and dark." Addie looked at him like a helpless child, forehead scrunched fighting tears, nodding her head. "Grab your suit, corral the girls, I'll catch up."

Relieved, Adelaide set the half empty coffee cup in the sink and looked out at the water. Three foot swells, not too rough, excellent conditions for the twins. Max might even join. She rushed to the twin's room, they'd been moping all morning, playing games on their phones. They were dressed and ready to leave. "Hey, lose the phones, find your suits, surf's up." Zelda shot Trudy a look. Trudy shrugged, mouthed the words, *she's nuts*. She made a circling gesture with her index finger, and kept right on playing. "Gertrude, you have three minutes to turn that thing off, find your suit and head to the beach. We're staying."

Adelaide pivoted on her heels halfway out the door, sticking her head back in,

"I saw that." She doesn't give a shit, she's too happy. She hears the girls giggling, unzipping bags, phones powering down. Life was simple here. There were no schedules to manage, rearrange, after school activities, carpools, juggling, no infuriating Smart phones. Smart phones make people stupid, and they were stupid enough. The Cove was pure oxygen, sun and sea.

Maxine. If she couldn't fix the tantrum queen tradition, she sure as hell could postpone it. "We're not leaving Max," Addie yells from the hallway, not bothering to stop. She knew Max would be pleased, like her mama. Now, Georgia. Addie scurried off towards the den where Zack used to sleep. Adelaide stopped short of the French doors and gasped. Georgia was perched on the crackled, faded leather sofa wearing her grandfather's favorite ripped, cream woolen cardigan, the one with brown elbow patches and moth holes that Harry had threatened to toss. Georgia sat hugging her knees, blank stare, empty, emerald eyes. She must have dug through the garment bags and pulled out the sweater when they packed his things. Her sorbet splatter paint baby, feisty girl went missing.

The room was cold and vacant. Addie felt a chill on this golden ball, indigo sky, optimum 75 degrees, Cali beach day. Sunny childhood days flooded back, she woke delirious, flying through the kitchen, grabbing an apple, out the screen porch, snatching her board and wetsuit from the hook, descending the concrete slabs two at a time. Into the ocean in under three minutes, her mother kept time on the chalkboard that hung in the kitchen. 2:32, 2:48, 1:52. She'd forgotten about that, where was her mother now? Addie knew it was her turn to keep count and she hated it. Being a mother is hard. She'd been a real shit to Harry. Addie figured it was her turn to bite down. She swallowed air and went in.

"Babe," tread lightly. Nothing, Georgia was blank. Addie was terrified, didn't dare move. She tiptoed to the floral chaise, opposite the couch. "GEORGIA PINE," she spoke in a deep, stern voice, one of authority Georgia would recognize. The stupor broke, Addie moved to the couch. Not too close, she did not touch her daughter. Georgia processed in her own time.

Adelaide understood and respected her boundaries, relieved to be close, in proximity.

"We're staying. Sound good." Georgia sat up straight, turned to face her striking, strong, capable mother and knew. *This* was going to hurt. "I'm not going back."

Adelaide wasn't in shock. She should have been furious, sad, wounded, all the hideous emotions a mother experiences losing a child. She was losing her, no longer able to insulate her from the crapshoot world. She rationalized; this was completely natural, part of the deal. Being her mother, birthing, nurturing, disciplining, mending, loving and letting go. She knew. She'd done the same to her mom. She knew. Georgia was walking before she could stand, and sprinting five minutes later. The early years, Addie's only objective was keeping her child alive. Georgia left her the second she was born. She knew in her mind, her heart lagging behind. She couldn't be over emotional, heartbroken and recently depleted. Her father took a piece of her heart when he died, one she would never grow back. Addie knew, before Georgia left Maine, before her father, before the unpredictable storm summer. Adelaide understood because she *knew* Georgia Pine. She prayed she'd come back. Why does he/she/whoever do it? She wondered. Not even remotely religious, Adelaide believed in the currents. Why does he give us *so* much love, only to steal it back? She hoped she loved Georgia big, wise, and kind enough. Prayed she'd been mother enough.

"Okay, then." Adelaide slapped her knees, leaned in and pecked her cheek. "I'm surfing with your sisters. You know where to find us." Ouch. Casting the freedom line. That stings.

There is something about a seashore dwelling, how the wind blows steady, sweeping and swooshing problems away. They magically evaporate out to sea. Harry couldn't know how blessed time and living inside that house would be. The home was evergreen, oversized planks, cool to the touch but so very warm inside. The picnic bench carved with etched markings, familiar names, some recent, others worn. Barely legible grooves recorded a family. Nothing special, comfy rockers keep time on the front porch. Crickets wait by the window to lull you to sleep. Sweet honeysuckle and magnolia trees satiate the senses, easing worry and heightening dreams. The Cove is no ordinary home, the sacred sanctuary alive, where hope resides, abundant. The waves in perpetual movement invite love.

Punch Line

X felt for this family. When they hurt, rejoiced, loved, fought, she cried. She couldn't control her feelings, used the words to release exaggerated emotions. Her head knew they weren't real, never mattered to her heart. She was alive in their world, consumed by the living details. X submersed herself in the Cove. On that magical beach, she could feel the hot granules of sand between her toes, muscles burn from the walk, run barefoot, dance and swim. With Harrison close, she had two legs, feet and toes, a healed body. She understood she was writing for the girl, Opal. Seven, whoever she was. Tread lightly, she thought. She was scared, too deep in it. Loosing Harrison once almost killed her. Stupid, she really thought this time would be different. She was so stupid. Writing came easy for X, until she was done. She retreated, recoiled for weeks, months. Saying good-bye to character creations she adored was excruciating. She gave them fragments, hope and her most intimate, private parts. She would not lose her a second time. The grief was real, palpable. Harrison could stay with her, she had space in her mind. Holding onto Harry was the domino effect; she kept the Cove alive, Harrison, Zack and Addie's family fell in line. Losing her mother was black nothingness. The one story she couldn't hide behind.

Torn Ligaments

Today was not a day of firsts. There had been so many life firsts, Addie stopped to look up. She did not want to miss one; with four babies there had been multitudes. The daughter responsible for making Addie a mother when she was barely an adult, Georgia showed her how. When she wasn't doing it right, testing her to be better, stronger, more patient. She made life easier for her sisters, by default. Addie made mistakes with her firstborn, she could not fix. This was a different kind of firsts. Leave it to Georgia to hurt her heart without meaning to. Addie needed the extra days at the Cove to do nothing. Feel the sun; remember how much her mother loved it. When Addie asked if she missed Hollywood, fame, Harry laughed, shaking her head. "God, no. I got all this," twirling round and round, stretching her arms towards the beach, house, sky, running her fingers through Adelaide's mane. She knew with her whole heart that Harrison meant it. Addie sighed. She was leaving her quasi adult-child behind, her precocious, ginger. This was not a first. This was an *unfirst*, experiences they would share separately, living apart. Georgia would have to hold her mother's hand, ever so gently letting go.

Five Million Reasons

Bags packed, bills settled, Zack's affairs in order, Adelaide had run out of excuses. Time to go, the twins had school, practice. Maxine would be a senior, college prep maybe. Addie couldn't convince her, Max had a different plan. Since she was stuck to the kitchen floor in fetal position, Addie knew Max would wear her down. Besides, Maxine was the responsible one, the one she worried least about. She needn't worry, Maxine was born independent, when she wasn't glued to the outdated linoleum, kitchen floor.

"Max, you're being ridiculous. Three minutes." Their ride would be there any minute. Georgia offered to drive them to the airport, her mother refused. A sappy, drawn out good-bye, no thank you. She wanted the hell out while she had the nerve. The kitchen floor looked awfully appealing. Addie stepped over Max, peaked out the kitchen window. She hated leaving the Cove on a sunny day. This was her refuge, her safe place. It was home, even after two decades and a Maine driver's license. Caden promised they'd move back, someday. They didn't. They weren't empty promises, he meant it and so had she. Family shifted priority, they adapted. The girls thrived in Maine; relatives, cousins and friends kept them busy. Theirs was a happy house, dining table cluttered with projects, little humans running through the rooms, yummy smells from the oven. It was a full life, Addie was lucky. Caden was a wonderful partner, friend and father. She couldn't split with her backpack anymore when life got messy. She had serious baggage, complete with titanium nametags. Her babies were her happy place, grounding, earth reality. She counted on the much needed respite come summer, six weeks in paradise. Her personal, sea shine break from the monotony that comes with children. Georgia and Caden sat on the picnic table, mirroring one other. Deep in conversation, Georgia listened intently to her father. She was playing with her hair, a bad habit inherited from her mother. Addie's head bobbled unaware, sucking back tears. Caden would calm her, say what Georgia needed to hear. He had a way with her, one she never had. He'd come home from work, throw his coat on the rack, missing, ending up on the floor, loosen his tie and scoop a screaming baby from her playpen. Within minutes, she'd be cooing and smiling. Made Addie furious, until Max was born. 6:00 o'clock could not come fast enough. Harry helped, until she couldn't stand the commotion. "I'm a grandmother, I get to leave. Take this child, for the love of *Christ*. I need a nap." Addie smiled at the memory of her movie star mother, spit up on her shirt, hair sticking straight up, completely disheveled. That was the best, making her mother nuts. Georgia's fiery hair cascading down Caden's back, her head resting on his shoulder. Addie felt like a thief, stealing an intimate moment that did not belong to her. Georgia had not yet discovered how stunning and courageous she'd become. The insecurity curse dissipates with age, the women in her family unique, pure beauty possessed at birth. She had no doubt when Georgia opened her heart, she would discover the courage, strength, guts and exquisiteness she owned, from day one. When Addie handed Georgia the envelope from her grandparents on Zack's beat up couch, Georgia studied her mother's eyes. She opened the envelope slowly, meticulously. No longer her child, barely an adult, Georgia held the weight of responsibility in her hands. The same weight Adelaide felt when Harry gave Addie her own freedom and autonomy she had not earned. You are expected to stand on your own, yet no one gets through life alone. Funny, polar opposites collide. Whatever Georgia decides, however she spends the dough, Addie would be watching fingers crossed. Biting her nails, losing sleep and praying to a God she does not believe in. Georgia opened the letter, took her time reading each word, every sentence and read it again. She looked at her mother, panic and shock. Adelaide stroked her hair reassuring her daughter this was happening.

"What am I supposed…FIVE MILLION DOLLARS," Georgia blurted, barely able to speak. Addie continued stroking her hair, calming her down.

"Something good, with purpose. Freedom and no puppet strings. That's what Harry wanted, your grandfather agreed."

Georgia's brain was spinning, unable to process. She rubbed her temples, standing. Pacing, letter in hand, Addie knew her spitfire daughter was dumb-funded. That rarely happened. Georgia was black or white, watching her in the gray zone was a relief. She was not taking things lightly. "Pops wanted you to take care of the Cove. Watch over the house, love her as much as they had. Your sisters, Dad and I have life visitation rights of course. Would you do that, for him? You don't have to. You can say no. The money? Tucker's son will advise you."

"UGH, Stinko? Gross." Tucker used to bring him to the beach, to picnics, to surf. Kids bullied him at school, he was awkward, a little fat. They were kids, how could she remember him? Adelaide chuckled; he had been an ugly, pimply kid with bad hygiene.

"I hear he's a wiz, Hollywood's A-listers' hot shot lawyer. Call, his name's Dash, not Stinko."

Georgia shook her head, hysteria hit, fell back on the couch and kicked her feet in the air. Letting loose, releasing the absurdity she felt. Her grandmother was a frigging' movie star who gave away a fortune. "El Stinko!"

"Georgia, do something for me?" Georgia half laughing and crying, throws her arms up in defeat. "*Do* from the heart, not your stubborn head. And, go a little crazy. It's OK to be reckless. I know, big contradiction. We put restrictions on you in high school; we had to. Lose them. You've been squashed long enough."

"Who are you, and where is my high-strung mother?" Georgia rolls her eyes, change, don't change. She's miffed, the woman is nuts.

"I'm you, in this exact spot twenty years ago. No kids, husband, just me. For a brief, charmed minute, I was free. That envelope changed my insulated world, zero decisions, money, a backpack and a first class experience. You will never have this day, this hour, this opportunity, ever again. Trust me, you'll be *me* soon enough."

Georgia awkwardly threw her arms around her mother. Georgia's gesture was precisely what her mother needed to go home. Knowing in her heart her precocious, fierce girl would be just fine. Adelaide looked up from the dishes in the sink, reliving the past weeks. The immeasurable pain of losing her father would follow her to Maine. She was leaving Georgia behind. As she watched Caden with their baby, how gentle his mannerisms, delicate touch, she was overwhelmed. The Cove was not some bungalow in need of fixing, coat of paint; it was a home where magic lived. Every corner infused with a mother's courage to choose love. A love so big it permeated the walls. Addie understood her mother better, picking Zack and her child was never a choice at all. It was the wisest, bravest decision Harry made. Standing on creaky floors in that outmoded 80's kitchen, she would not change one knob, not one small detail. That home, that family, her infuriating, fierce, loyal, overbearing mother chose well.

You know I'd rather be surfing than praying. I never looked farther than the sea for answers, trusting the riptides and currents. Maine was not where I thought I'd be, my heart had a different geography in mind. I have no regrets because of you, a mother with backbone who knew when to cast, and when to reel me in. I miss you, it can't be, twenty years? I hear your voice. I see you laughing and dancing with daddy, colored lights dangling in the trees, music drifting from the house. Your gypsy child spinning round and round, barefoot, wild gold mane in love with her mommy and daddy. Your pretty face, shiny baldhead wrapped in dignity. Me sobbing under the covers in your bed, you brushing the tears away, cupping my face in your hands. When I close my eyes, I still feel them. Warm, comforting hands. It was a wonderful life, our cocoon. I pray I did half the job as well as you, with my little humans. I'm terrified, sometimes. It's your voice that scolds, the one I hear. I picture your statuesque frame standing on shore, annoyed, hands on hips. Your enormous, ridiculous, floppy beach hat casts an evening shadow. "Adelaide, enough water. Out, dry off. I'm not kidding." I don't want to go. I want to stay right here, everything exactly the way it was. My stomach hurts each time we pack. It's ridiculous, I know. All the love that came after started here, in this home. They're leaving, mom. One by one, I can't stop it. It's inevitable. I wish you could see them, my girls. Independent, quirky, quasi grown, they take my breath away. On the precipice of who they'll love, all they will experience, who they will become. I can't believe you're not here savoring this, barking orders. Take care of sweet Georgia Pine, our girl. Check in from time to time, you and daddy. Thank you mama, for all that I have, and all that I am.

Adelaide watches Georgia turn towards the drive. Caden stands, stretches his gangly arms and legs, looks in the same direction. Addie grabs the towel, dries her hands, folding it over the dish rack. "Girls. Car's here, Max get off the floor. " Adelaide's carry-on sits waiting on the screen porch. She takes a look around, makes a mental checklist what needs to be done. Forgetting for half a second that Georgia would be there to take care of whatever needs doing. She'd figure it out. Max, Trudy and Z-Z appear on the porch, carry-ons, Smartphones, headphones and sunglasses, airport ready. They look worse than their mother, the twins had been crying and Max could not get any paler. "Hey, what's with the sour pusses? Z, you have your own room, finally." Zelda shakes her head, erupting with tears. Addie opens her arms wide, embracing the three of them. "Don't, chicklets. You can chat, Skype every day, whatever you kids do. It's time."

Adelaide was a big fat liar, she knew she lied to her daughters. Life would be *Georgiaadventure -less*, she wasn't fooling. "Hug your sister. Car. Let's go." Adelaide watched Georgia, fiery, drop dead daughter in blue jean cutoffs, gypsy top and clogs twirl a strand of crimson, flowing locks lit from behind. She stood stoic, smiled, hugging and playfully kissing the twins. Max, dressed in sweats stood behind her boisterous sisters, awkwardly waiting her turn. Georgia gently raised Maxine's chin looking through her eyes. Georgia whispered in Max's ear, Max giggled and held tight to her protector. Maxine released the death grip, grabbed her bags, and bolted for the SUV. Georgia shuffled her feet, searching for her mother. Georgia found her, and locked eyes. She was scared; Adelaide felt it. She had to be strong, for both of them. Addie walked to her child, relaxed and confident. Georgia's body settled. "You got this, it's fine. We'll call." Georgia nodded. Adelaide hugged her, pecked her cheek, mussed her hair and turned away, gritting her teeth.

"Hey, mom. I hear clenching will give you lock jaw." Addie laughed, waving her off without turning around. She must have said that a thousand times when Georgia had a mouth full of expensive metal. She knew her baby was smiling, Addie didn't need to turn back. She slid across the cool leather next to her husband, checked the girls were settled in back. Caden squeezed her hand; Adelaide squeezed back. "We're set, we can go." She meant it.

Clickety-Clack

X was overtired. A postcard of the Bay Bridge arrived yesterday, with the word, KOOL!!! Signed, XO Seven. She was pushing hard, for her. Amped morning routines, in the chair fast, ready to work. Skipping sponge baths when she could. She didn't use plot outlines, set self-induced deadlines on a calendar. This book was beating the crap out of her, physically and emotionally. There were too many characters, intersecting plots, her head spun. She wrote all day, skipping lunch. The editors were pissed; she hadn't sent pages, progress reports. Fuck that, and fuck them. Not this one, this was for *her,* and Opal. She didn't care if it sold a copy, only needed one or two. She typed, ignoring her publisher's SHOUTY CAP emails. X was drained, obsessed and delirious. Lost and found in worlds she invented. Living outside the burn felt so good. She should eat better, take vitamins and a power nap. Yeah, so not happening. Damn it all to hell, X was hooked. She never knew where the characters were going, there was no master plot. The point came where she sat back, no longer in charge. She trusted her characters; they were her phantom limbs. It was the one place X didn't doubt. Didn't feel the excruciating pain, or realize her legs were gone. In that chair, the parallel universe of her doing, she hoped some of the magic rubbed off. The punctual dark appeared to remind her it had not. Sounds crazy, if she kept typing she had a shot. Hating herself a little less.

Green Envy

Georgia lay on the picnic table, ginger hair swaying, keeping time with the breeze, sweeping the grass and dirt below. It grew long and wild, lightened by too much time in the sun and saltwater. She thought she'd be sad when they left, she wasn't. She felt lighter, free. Her sisters weren't bugging her, fighting over some idiot boy, crying, slamming doors. She didn't take three-minute showers, afraid the hot water would run out. Her happy bubble was serene. Georgia worried she'd be scared in the house on her own. Weird sounds, prowlers, creepy crawlers. Instead, she slept soundly. She went weeks without checking her phone or a clock, days without washing. She woke, made coffee, packed fruit, nuts, whatever was on the table, went to the beach, hung with the locals, smoked weed, surfed, napped, meditated and watched a sunburst orange, yellow sun disappear behind the ocean, guessing which fantastic hues it would leave behind. Legs crossed, in her striped string bikini, body lithe and tan, fiery tresses touching her butt. The dazzling, young woman sitting yoga style where dry sand meets the tide, was breathtaking. Georgia like her grandmother, never gave her beauty a thought. Bowing her head, hands in prayer in front of her heart. She silently thought of her family, pops and Harry, offering gratitude. Even if she wasn't feeling particularly grateful, figured it couldn't hurt. Georgia reached for the tissue soft, frayed, baby blue sarong tying it tight around her waist. She packed her wetsuit, mom's tangerine board, Klean Kanteen, SPF30, IPod and various crap, starting the trek up to the house. Her body was fit, lean and tan from hours at the beach. She detested gyms, creeps and posers on machines going nowhere. Why the hell would she do that? Stairs she snickered as she climbed, muscles tighter with each step. The hotter the burn, the faster she climbed. Georgia turned when she reached the top, habit. Half expecting to see *him* smiling from the beach, waving. Each night the postcard panoramic, coastal view stunned her; the beauty was terrifying. Georgia was afraid of one thing. No other place would feel like this. Why would anyone leave, ever? Even without her grandfather, Harry, parents and sisters around, Georgia felt whole. She didn't want to share her secret with anyone. Hanging her wetsuit and towel on hooks to dry, propping the board against the house, she checked her gardens before dark. Georgia became quite the master gardener, complete with a raised, irrigated vegetable garden. Weeding, hoeing, watering, pruning, Georgia made a mental list of supplies. She used the same nursery pops had driven her to countless times. She cut magnolia for a vase, she loved the clean, sweet scent permeating the house. Suddenly starving, weed and surfing does that. Georgia grabbed a wicker basket filling it with fresh carrots, Vidalia onion, fennel, bell pepper, arugula, spinach and ripe, Sunset heirloom tomatoes. She snickered whenever somebody proclaimed they ate *'organic.'* They'd never heard the term *Monsanto*. Georgia rolled the hose, put away the shears, locked the shed for the night. She loved evenings, gathering her basket of colors and flowers, the garden never felt like a chore. She took her time trimming and arranging the flowers. Placing a tall, round vase on the kitchen table, a thin, glass one on the nightstand by the bed. She brushed her teeth, flossed and washed her face, smelling her pits. Didn't stink, she'd shower tomorrow. She was in saltwater all day, way better for your skin. Georgia changed into an oversized white tee, flannel sweats, *aka* her pajamas. She laid the fruits and veggies on the kitchen counter, methodically washing, dicing and chopping. She made a massive, mouthwatering salad, added Parmesan, pine nuts and pink tuna. Snatched gluten-free crackers, tap water and sat down to a feast. She wasn't scared one bit. Georgia loved her life at the Cove, it was full on repetition that wasn't monotonous at all. Satiated, she finished the kitchen cleanup, and turned out the light. Grabbing pop's tattered cashmere cardigan, she went outdoors. The picnic table was where she ended the day, night after night. The air was chilly, her exposed toes and tip of her nose were blue. The table was wet with dew. She sprawled out. She was glad she brought the sweater. The endless, cowboy blue sky shared by the half crescent moon, was blanketed in sparkling lights. That sky, this perfect day, tranquil, breezy night was exactly how she pictured heaven. Tomorrow, she'd have *sex*. Not here, never the house. Any of the dudes were fine, as long as it was quick, no hassle. She didn't want her first to be someone she loved, who could squash her. She wanted someone *totally* forgettable. It was settled under a Cove night sky and cluster of stars. Georgia would get laid, shower, head to the nursery and call el Stinko. He'd been hassling her for months. Best to get that handled before her mom drove her bonkers. Georgia was sleepy but not tired. She rested her eyes two seconds, tucked into a caterpillar cocoon, content as she drifted.

Whoop Dee Do

Georgia uncovered Zack's Chevy, the one he had hidden, had refused to give up when his eyes gave out, and his daughter pleaded. No way, parked behind the shed was his independence, his dignity protected by commercial plastic. Georgia swung the tarp over the fence and hopped in, dust filling her nostrils. She loved that old thing; he taught her to drive stick. Addie begged her daughter to sell it, wasn't safe, blah, blah, blah. True to Harrison form, NO meant no. Sandwiched between stubborn and stubborn, her mother knew when to push, and when it was useless. Her pops made sure Georgia knew her way under a hood, change a flat, oil check, rudimentary. Car stuff most women never bothered with. Georgia wasn't *most* women. She manually rolled the squeaky windows down, turning the key. Hiking boot on the clutch in beat up camos, she popped the clutch satisfied, down shifted into reverse backing out the long driveway and up the hill. The metal antenna found two radio stations, country and pop. Country, windows down, hair flying, Georgia loved the scenic drive on the Pacific Coast Highway to *her* nursery. She almost forgot she popped her cherry. Whoever said sex was this spiritual, cosmic, amazing experience was bonkers. It was messy, ew and yuck. Flat on her back, hidden behind huge, pointy rocks that stuck in her shoulder blade, so not pleasant. Zuma boy wouldn't brag. He had a serious, not so serious girlfriend. Predictable, hot, shit for brains, super-annoying celebrity daughter. Total lameness. Sex was awkward.

Jacqueline Cioffa

Georgia was indifferent. She signaled turning into her second most favorite place, *MaliBeau Nursery*. She parked the truck and stepped inside the enchanted green garden, alive with form, scent, magnificent flora in varying weird shapes and sizes. Her sunbeam eyes skimmed California Poppy, Chaparral Honeysuckle, Snapdragon, Manzanitas and Hummingbird Sage. She headed for the restroom before pulling out her list, running into Jake. Jake, the owner's son with flaxen hair, grey wolf-envy eyes, perfect jaw line, rugged model looks and cheeky grin. Goddamn, he was something. He greeted Georgia with a friendly, bear hug. Jake was sticky, smelled like dirt in the best possible way.

"Hey you. We were getting ready to uh…*worry*?" shaking his head an exaggerated no. Georgia playfully slapped his bicep, "crazy busy, doing nothing. You remember."

"Ah, not really." Jake was thirtyish, Georgia guess-timated. He'd worked there since her first visit with pops. It was a family business, and he was the only son. Georgia discovered this on the third visit after grilling him, spitfire teenager and all. Jake never got riled, he teased. "Some of us have a *job*," winking, hoisting a forty pound bag of Biodegradable to his shoulder.

"Come find me, I want to run something by you." Georgia pointed to the restroom, holding up two fingers. A decade of dance between them, he knew exactly where she was going without the hand gesture. Was she *that* predictable? She thought she was so mysterious; maybe she was not. She was super curious, what could he want? She'd learned not to overthink Jake. He might be the only person she ever met in the *entire state* of California, who didn't have an agenda. Jake was Jake, talked with his mouth not from his ass. Jake was half the reason she drove the extra hour. The other shop had the best product, but he was living green *before* there was green living. Georgia peed fast, finger combed her hair, twisting it into a bun. Scouting for Jake, he spotted her first, whistled. Georgia giggled, that's how her grandfather used to find her, pigtails, shorts, firecracker weaving between the shrubs, lost in green envy gardens. Zack would look worried when she finally came skipping out, exotic flower in hand. Not Jake, he was amused. "I can pay," Georgia retorted. Waving the exotic purple branch, reaching in her back pocket.

"I'll put it on your tab. If you're going to snatch a flower that pretty, better learn her name." Jake needled Georgia, cheeks burnt red to match her tresses. Jake taught her about the earth, compost, organic pesticides, which plants thrive in the desert, by the beach, how to wait, watch and nurture. She was a master gardener yet still had so much room to grow. She tapped his shoulder from behind. "Spill." Jake turned off the mister, removed his gloves, leaned against the table and crossed his boots. "We're building a sustainable garden in South Compty, nothing fancy, greens, some fruit, the basics, easy to manage. You can't be a surfer-stoner forever."

"Why the hell not? I excel at it," secretly thrilled that he asked.

"I need someone I can trust, who knows what they're doing. I got five guys, two trucks lined up, we'll do the grunt work. Show up, that's all. Wednesday noon, 15 Compty, empty lot."

Georgia chewed her bottom lip, freeing her hair, twirling a strand. *"Come on, Jesus Jake."*

"Bring your gloves and sunny, chirpy personality," kissing her cheek. "You are going to *love* it."

"Fine. We are so even." Georgia felt her cheeks getting hot, relieved he was already halfway down the aisle.

"Wednesday twelve o'clock, kid."

And there it was. Her happily ever after lost to a truckload of compost, dated ten-dollar dungarees and a shovel.

Brazuca Bebe

Addie checked the clock noting the time difference before dialing. Voice mail, again. She would wring Georgia's neck, little shit. In precisely five days, two hours and fifty minutes, they were meeting at JFK. During Gertrude's last semester of college while playing soccer in Madrid, she fell hard. Broke her ankle, squashing all chances to go pro. Six months of PT, grueling rehabilitation, bubbly Trudy was frustrated, deflated and depressed. She called weekly, begging her mom to let her come home. "Sorry honey, you'd forfeit the scholarship and not graduate."

"Christ," tossing the phone on the bed, storming around the dorm. Gertrude hobbled with a cane, filled with loathing and self-pity. Earphones blasting, she went to the gym pouting, sat on the warm up bed, annoyed that her trainer was late. She lay back, stretching her limbs, exaggerating each move. She was oblivious to her surroundings. Gertrude was not alone. He caught her eye in the dirty, skinny gym mirrors. Holy shit. Holy, holy, holy Nike. Sexy twelve pack, dark, emerald eyes, uncomfortably handsome *Madrid Really,* soccer superstar was amused by her antics. Trudy wasn't ugly exactly, she was ordinary attractive. Not bombshell pretty but with killer calves and an athlete's body. He hopped off the table limping in her direction. Crap, crap crappers. She hadn't bothered to wash her hair, apply concealer or put on gloss in weeks.

"Hola. I'm"...holding out his *ten million* dollar hand.

"Xavi," said the stuttering starstruck girl. "What happened?" pointing down.

"Nada, tight hamstring. Trainer's late, no. Hungry? Vamanos," reaching for her hand.

"I'm in gym shorts," protesting.

"You're perfect for me," towering over her.

"Huh? I'm starving," ignoring bad grammar, grabbing her cane. They passed the trainers in the hall; normally she'd turn back. Xavi squeezed her hand tight, kept on walking. No explanation, no excuse, just daylight where a hundred camera shutter clicks exploded in unison. She looked like shit; oh well. PT went from a Debbie downer to a number in the *infinities.*

Ten lunches, twenty dinners, one VIP soccer pass, a trip to Corsica, Trudy was cooked. Xavi was not the cocky, show glitz, all-star persona. He was a sweet, gentle Corsican farmer's son who adored his mama, and loved the game. He worked hard despite supreme talent, played smart since childhood. She couldn't be happier, feel any more loved than here, this moment, with this man. He was her first, his patient face showed her he understood this, his actions told her how much he cared. The semester was up; Trudy was in a panic. Now, God. NOW, really? You have got to be shitting. She couldn't leave, he hadn't *asked* her to stay. She needed her sister, she'd know. She tried Skype; Georgia never bothered to answer. Goddamn infuriating, pick up just this once.

Two days before death-day, Xavi was at a conference in Rome. Promised he'd be home that evening. Gertrude kept checking her Xavi cell. He gave her an iPhone, (*mini-computer*), so they could chat whenever, wherever. No texts, messages all day. By 6:00 o'clock she was beating the pillow with her fists, face down sobbing, boxes packed, suitcases smothering her. A knock at her door, she quickly wiped her wet face, smoothed her hair, flinging the door open, deflated. 7:00 o'clock, he wasn't coming. In a frenzy, furious, she didn't notice the garment bag hanging on the door with a note. *Put me on, downstairs, 8:00 o'clock.* Trudy unzipped the garment bag, gasping. Strapless, miles and miles of intricate, gold beads blinded her. Armani. It belonged on a six foot glamazon at a red carpet event, not *her*. She beamed; there were strappy gold heels and a matching gold clutch in the bottom of the bag. Holy shit, probably cost more than a small home. When Adelaide handed her daughter 'the envelope' she had refused. The baby, she knew what was coming, her sisters had big mouths. She asked her mom to keep it safe; she wasn't ready. Addie was secretly thrilled her baby wasn't in a rush to grow up and leave. Gertrude emptied the contents of her purse on the bed, scouring what little makeup she owned. She washed her face, combed her hair pinning it back. She went through *beauty basic boot camp,* taught by her sisters. Cream, shimmer eye shadow (not too much), bronzer/pink blush combo, lash curler, waterproof mascara, concealer and lipstick. Luckily her skin was blemish free, golden-brown from Corsica; she skipped foundation. Moisturize, slip the dress on bottom to top. It weighed a thousand pounds of opulence, Wizard of Oz heels, full-length mirror check. Trudy gasped at the stunning woman. So, that's how beautiful feels. Wow, the dress belonged in a high art museum. Relieved her ankle was healed, and the stilettos weren't sky high. Ten 'till; clutch, credit card, cash, gloss and keys, check.

Her classmates gawked when she floated down the hall. Nervous stomach, she knew this was all him. Still. She spotted his driver standing by the car and waved. He grinned like a teenager, opening her door. "Preciosa, senorita."

"Gracias," her limited vocabulary of a year abroad.

When they pulled up to the Ritz by Belmond, a young man greeted her, extending his arm. In perfect English he said, "You look exquisite Miss Gertrude, your party is waiting."

Trudy had no idea what he was thinking; she was trembling. "Have a delightful evening, Senora." When the young man released her arm, guiding her inside the lavish banquet room, overflowing with exotic floral arrangements, pink champagne flutes, flickering white candlelight, Trudy was overwhelmed by the beauty. Her gown flashed shimmering golden facets whenever she moved. Expecting Xavi to collect her, she could not find him in the umber glow of the room. She felt the lightest tap on her shoulder, swinging around.

"Hi, baby. You are magnificent."

"Daddy?!"

Gertrude cried, throwing her arms tight around her father. He was really there, holding her. They all were, mom, Georgia, Maxine and Z-Z, bursting, drinking pink champagne with mini hamburgers. Zelda rushed to embrace her twin, the sister mirror she adored. "Trudy, I could not love you more. I miss you *too* much." Gertrude, wiser by seven minutes and forty seconds, "don't cry silly, you'll muss the makeup." They giggled in sync. Georgia looked ravishing, hair long, loose and beachy, made up in an emerald, silk dress. Xavi's proud parents nodded, mama blew her a kiss. She felt him before she saw him, in a neat black suit and skinny tie, standing alone near the balcony, looking pleased. Trudy sprinted, not caring if it was *un*ladylike. She could not stand one more second. Xavi swept her off the ground, drawing her close. Whispering in her ear, "I could not watch you go."

In a whirlwind *fiesta* weekend, complete with family, Gertrude got engaged, married (permission asked and granted) and Lear jetted to Bali, not back to Maine. Not before saying goodbye to her family, hard tears and happy goodbyes.

"The second I met you and every second in between, you make me so proud. My baby." Her mother promised no wasted tears, it was Spain, an *unfirst*. In Addie's family Gertrude was the easy baby, smiling child who made life fun. She would miss her gigantic heart, infectious enthusiasm. Zelda would not say goodbye to her double, souls split down the middle. She motioned Trudy cupping her ear, "You might have gotten married first, but I'm having a baby. *Shhh*, secret." They always traded secrets, the twins created a world all their own. "*YOU* stinker," Trudy and Zelda giggled like adolescents at a slumber party. Z-Z was in love with her college sweetheart, studying to be a professor like dad. She loved Maine; would never leave and didn't want to. Zelda was more than fine, she was happy at home. "I'll be there, no worries."

"I'm no dummy. I know," planting a kiss on her sister's cheek. Georgia was Georgia, without the bite. "I love you, Georgia Pine. Thanks for never picking up." Georgia held Gertrude's arms staring into her gentle eyes speaking softly, "you never needed me, you were born sensible. You tell dark and handsome, I will cut off his priceless feet if he…"

"Georgia, enough! We'll come. I want to show him the Cove. Answer the damn phone, will 'ya."

"We'll see, think lover boy can handle a board," winking.

Maxine was strange the entire weekend, painfully quiet. Gertrude worried. Max seemed even more withdrawn than usual. Gertrude wanted to get her alone; it never happened. Max would open up to her. Addie told her not to fret, worry was a mother's job. She would take care of Maxine. Still, something felt wrong. Trudy tried to shrug the bad off; this was a happy time.

She thanked her broken ankle daily. Never complained when it rained and her arthritic foot throbbed. Sixty plus years of wonderful lay ahead, three children and five grandchildren. Gertrude had a solid marriage, loved her life and learned Spanish. Eventually.

Xavier promised mom and dad, he'd take good care of her. They would visit Maine often. Gertrude never missed *her* family, because her husband kept *his* word.

Miss Barbara

Georgia did not want to get lost in Compty. Not because she was afraid, or some bullshit like that. She hated wasting time stuck in the car. Which was ironic, life in LA meant living in your car. She dreamt of foreign plains and adventures, Joshua Tree, City of Rocks, New Mexico, Louisiana Bayous, Austin, Louisville. Live on a hundred acre ranch complete with a bright, yellow barn, geldings and mares, Australian Shepherds running free. The smoking hot, rancher dude, sprig of grass between his teeth, smiling under his cowboy hat. Desert terrain, tumbleweed isolation, sticky Bayou, sweet mystery, dry heat novelty enticed her. New, something different. The Cove, salt air, gardens, her easy life kept her in Cali. Georgia could not reconcile the two. She'd pack the truck and go. Someday. There'd be time. She spotted Jake's trucks, drove around the block three times, a silver Volvo was pulling out and floored it. Pleased, Georgia did a two second visor mirror check, grabbed her beat up Stalwart garden bag, swung it over one shoulder and locked the truck. Jake was preoccupied helping the guys, his trusty notepad sticking out of his butt pocket. He was so stupidly unaware of his good looks, it was infuriating. When would she stop feeling like a ten year old with a silly crush? He'd never see her any differently, some code of honor. Georgia couldn't help whom she loved, even if they didn't love her back. That day, walking into the sweltering, empty asphalt lot would alter her core, paths shifting. Life would be thrown completely off course, in the absolute best, most meaningful direction. Jake was not her love, exactly. He was the conduit to her best self, his smirking grin and kind heart would be close forever.

Georgia opened her bag, pulled out working gloves and got busy building the beds, complete with an irrigation system. The men could haul the dirt. It was noon before she even looked up, shit it was hot. She was a sweaty, dirty mess. Georgia grabbed her green bandana, walked towards the hose, let it run until it was bone cold and dunked her dirty, fire engine locks shaking her head like a wet dog. That was better. She wet the bandana, wiped her hands, face and tied it around her head. She heard hoots and hollers, children laughing. That's when she looked. A brown skinned lady with cropped bleach blond hair, carrot color acrylics, horn rim glasses, smacked the back of the head of the boy next to her.

"Yes, ma'am." the sulking boy retreated, he looked around ten-*ish,* Georgia guessed. He was scared of the overpowering woman in the best possible way to be scared of an elder. She demanded respect. He wore his jeans low, kept hiking them up with a 3XXL short-sleeve, black tee, swoosh high tops and a frayed red baseball cap. Georgia hadn't noticed the two or three other boys, fold up table, pitchers of lemonade, cooler filled with sandwiches. She was under the spell of the larger than life character motioning her. Mystery woman smiled. Georgia smiled back, walking towards the enigma. The lady extended her long, bright coral acrylic nails, hand trailing behind. Georgia reached over the table to meet it. That handshake told Georgia everything she would come to know and love deeply about this woman. She was black, Georgia was white, there was no divider between them, except that plastic table.

"Hi, I'm Georgia." Georgia felt immediately happy and at ease in her presence.

"Miss Barbara." It said enough. They'd have time to pass the hours, shoot the shit, laugh, become true friends. Separated by a world of circumstance, color, racial barriers, Miss Barbara saw only who was standing in front of her. The wet mop, good intentioned, scraggly, gangly white girl. The faintest whimper came from under a shaded tree directly behind her. Miss Barbara obscured her view of a sleeping infant in its stroller. Not intentionally, no, not on purpose. The precious, baby boy opened his transparent butternut eyes, stretched out his edible chunk arms, clapping, razor focus on Georgia. She felt dizzy and sick, wanted to run. Georgia got chills in ninety degree, asphalt heat. Miss Barbara steadied her, holding her arm ever so gently, the exact way her mother would.

"Some sugar, sugar," pouring pink lemonade into a red, plastic cup. Georgia nodded grateful, her fate held in the firm handshake.

She was intrigued. Georgia got in her truck every night at twilight, made the hour trek to sit on a cement bench with Miss Barbara. She was fascinating, raising her son's kids with a stern voice and steady hand. He was dead, heroin overdose, mother in prison dealing crack. Miss Barbara never apologized; she was as transparent as the paper curtains hanging from busted windows.

"*You* are white, and *I* am black," Georgia joked. It was the truth, she was dark and Miss Barbara was light. The two older boys ignored the whack white lady, kicked around a soccer ball. If they got too loud, rowdy, Miss Barbara shot one look, raised an extra long, fake fingernail. They stopped. Miss Barbara nudged Georgia, whispering, "got 'ta be tough. Boy needs a mother and a father. I'm it." Georgia understood perfectly. Miss Barbara was the most brutally honest person she had ever met, besides Harry. Before she knew what Miss Barbara was up to, Jax was in her lap. Each visit, Georgia became more and more attached. He was the most irresistible, sticky sweet baby, and she hated kids. Chubby cheeks, soft skin, Georgia had to pry his tiny arms from around her neck. He screamed when she freed his fingers. Georgia kissed his cheek, eyes, nose and forehead before reluctantly handing him over. Before each visit she couldn't wait to see his smiling face, felt physically ill when she had to leave. Jax, her darling baby boy, was *the* man in her life.

Sustainable gardens and unbreakable promises were made that day.

Harry's Digs

Part of Harrison's trust helped Jake and Georgia build twenty thriving, sustainable gardens all over Los Angeles. She did not mind putting on a party dress, combing her hair, wearing a fake smile, use her grandmother's fame, attending some lame event, to raise more funds. Harry's Digs the green, non-profit business was born. Once the eco systems were built, beds, dirt, irrigation, fertilizer and seeds planted, the communities took over the daily maintenance. Everyone was welcomed and encouraged, 7 am – 5 pm. Georgia or Jake picked a point person who was *in charge*, kept an eye on the grounds, unruly teenagers, reeled up hoses, put the tools away, turned the water off and locked up at 5:00. The five o'clock curfew reduced vandalism, kept smart-ass punks out and drug dealers off the block.

Radicchio, spinach, escarole, vine tomatoes, carrots, onions, green beans, potatoes grew and thrived, feeding the disadvantaged. Not to mention the fruit beds. Once a garden became self-sufficient, Georgia and Jake stayed out of the way. Visiting only when there was a problem. Georgia had less time at the Cove to surf, hang at the beach, bummed for two seconds. She was feeding communities, something she had taken for granted. She couldn't remember one childhood belly rumble, an empty fridge. She'd been myopic, embarrassed by her cushy life. Mothers could send their kids to school with healthy, packed lunches. Their children wouldn't go to bed hungry. That felt awesome. She was glad Zack tore out the flowerbeds that she had loved, digging in the dirt. Her pops had been patient when she begged him to drive her to Jake's nursery. She was relieved she had gotten trouble out of her system early; now she had a decade of green living to keep her busy. She was always learning, nature was constantly evolving. Addie flew out, visited Harry's Digs with her very grown-up daughter.

Harrison would have beamed, bragging to Sofia and Katia. She had predicted Georgia would be the *independent woman, healer and fearless warrior. She was right, again.* Adelaide carried this child, yet Georgia continued to shock her. Addie hugged her firestorm, cherry vine girl tight, ignoring pre-set boundaries.

"Mom!" Georgia pulled away, secretly thrilled she had made her proud. Even grown up children seek their mama's approval. Every evening they returned to the beach, not wanting to miss the Cove's swirling, mystic sunsets. They prepared hearty salads from Harry's Digs basket of bounty adding pine nuts, almonds, egg, catch of the day. Adelaide was impressed, her daughter was well, a very capable young woman. Georgia lit tea lights in mason jars dangling precariously from rusted wire. Adelaide was heart happy, her parents alive in memory, every plywood crack, kitchen cupboard groove, stone step, sand granule, vintage board, chipped paint, the time capsule memory. Harry's rockers refinished long ago, Addie couldn't bear to fix the squeaky hinge on the front porch door. She'd miss the familiar sound each time it slammed, invoking childhood moments, teen angst, the ruler gauging the years. Georgia kept the house tidy, every cup, chair, bathroom towel in its proper place. She wondered if Georgia would tire of this place, life at the Cove, when the ache and itch might come. Addie studied the blissfully unaware creature lounging in the grass. Long limbs, surfer's body, mud under her fingernails. Georgia was pure, soft and hard, raw beauty contrasted by the tidal waves of crimson beach hair. She wondered why she'd been blessed with such a visceral creature with a defiant, questioning spirit. Ah, the women in her family, unique, magnificent, brazen beauties. She loved her daughters; Georgia, she loved separately. Spoiled, adored and loved by her own mother and father, she was the twine twisted between them. Her parents' true, all consuming love left an indelible imprint on her firstborn. Addie missed Harrison every day. A thousand little things over the course of her day she longed to share with her mother. There wasn't enough time. Funny, the irreplaceable things that go missing. The sorrow heavy with each milestone her girls lived, triumphs she could not share. The taken for granted times, like this, she missed her mother even more.

Addie wanted to be outdoors as much as possible, under a silver moon and incandescent sky, waves crashing below, air wet with salt tickling the skin, wind chimes playing her favorite melody. Relaxed, she sat at the picnic table absent-mindedly running her fingers across the familiar grooves, admiring the breathtaking night. She had returned to her most favorite, sacred place. You only get one heart happy home. This beach, her ocean, the funny, green clapboard house, was home. She wanted to die there, like her mother and father. She hoped later, not before she was finished watching her babes settle, content with families of their own. She was happy Caden packed her bag, pushing her out the door.

"Your to do-list can wait babe, go. She *asked* for you. In what universe does that happen?"

Adelaide spoke under breath, "In our shared universe, the mystic, magic Cove my love. Stubborn daughters need their mothers, beckoning them home." Tomorrow morning, Adelaide would pack her carry on and Georgia would drive her to the airport. She felt homesickness already creeping in, Addie was her truest self by the ocean.

Maine was where her people lived, her life full, duties, hobbies, the immaculate house where Caden would be waiting. Zelda was around the block, with a newborn. Addie should feel blessed, and she was. Mostly, she felt landlocked. She'd get up at dawn, and surf. Bottle the weightless feeling.

The ocean replenished her soul, she was the young, carefree girl again. It satisfied her, keeping desire and passion alive long after she settled back home. We can't fight the currents, Adelaide knew better. She embraced the gypsy and welcomed her true nature, the nomad she was inside. Hanging her wetsuit, racking her board she said, *see ya later*. Half of her heart stayed at the bluff, the other rolled her carry-on to the car. She got back to the business of being a mom.

She pecked her daughter on the cheek, "You done good, kid. We'll be back summertime. Call your sister." Georgia nodded, knowing exactly which sister she meant.

"Hey, thanks." Georgia could not say *the* words, her mother said them for her.

"I love you." Addie exited the car before Georgia saw her tears. God forbid the child witnessed emotion.

"I know." Georgia fixated on the steering wheel fidgeting with the sticky, torn leather, avoiding a drawn out, mush goodbye. Her mother knew better.

Adelaide hated flying, stirring up memories of *the* flight to Maine twenty years ago. The one she sobbed the entire five hours and twenty-six minutes. Tailwinds, her hands went numb, panic crawling beneath her skin. She passed out over Ohio, sniffling in her sleep. Poor schmuck next to her, he couldn't know it would be the last time she saw her bald, terminal mother. Harrison had held her, stroking her gold curls, wild mane. They managed goodbye; they would never be finished. No love letter, weeklong visit, puking shell of a fierce, brazen mother prepares you. She was there a second ago, in that house full of love. Young, stunning, cavorting on the beach, carrying her with toned, strong arms. Harrison wasn't the frail, cancer stricken, dying woman lying beside her in bed while Adelaide cried. Harry held her child's anguished face in her hands, brushing away her tears. Adelaide would never stop searching, talking, listening for her voice. Her mother couldn't, she was invincible. Dying, *her*? Impossible. She settled in her business class seat, unzipped her purse, took out Harry's black rimmed shades, now vintage. She didn't want anyone to see her tears, past or present. She hated good-byes as much as her willful daughter. She would hide the ugly cry, her pain from Georgia Pine. Shield the atrocities, whenever possible. Just like Harry had; knowing when to hold tight, tighter and when to shove her ass out the door. Because that's what mothers do. That's what good mothers do.

Blues Bayou

"Insanity runs in the family." Adelaide could not get Harry's words out of her head. Harrison's father died way before Zack or Addie were a concept. Her mom, right about the time she met Zack. Harry used to say all roads lead back, to Zack. She travelled, searched, sold her soul to stop fighting the currents. She didn't talk much about her past, how she had hopped a Greyhound. It wasn't a bad childhood, it was happy but also unbearably sad. It wasn't enough. At eighteen, foul mouth Harry wasn't settling. She got it all, Hollywood, fame, fancy cars, mansions, movie star envy, it sucked ass. *He* saved her. *Addie* saved her. Her grandbabies spit up saved her. Her soul sisters saved her. When Zack came out of the delivery room with the minutes old infant, Georgia, swaddled in his arms, Harry cried and cried. She could not stop crying. Zack sat next to his distressed love, these were not tears of joy. Their daughter's newborn asleep in his arms. "She's healthy, she's perfect. What?"

Harry did not stop sobbing, shaking her head, she would not look at her doting, patient, loving partner. She whispered heartbroken, "Insanity runs in the family." Zack's face creased. He knew Harrison's father had been ill, spent time in a mental ward. She told him, terrified, she spit it out, her whole story, even the parts she had omitted earlier. A West Hollywood night perfect for new lovers, the starlight, sweet breeze, gave Harry courage. She sat up in bed, just far enough from Pretty to talk.

She was falling hard, defining a relationship. The oh so confident young doctor knew, he loved all of her. He listened without interruption, her dad, how it broke him and shattered her family. How she would lock eyes, desperate to pull him out, bring him back from the nightmare he was stuck in. The crazy held him hostage behind dulled sunbeam hazel eyes, betrayed by his mind. Fucking disease. Harrison never gave up, he was in there fighting. She saw it, felt it with every molecule in her, her father was alive and well. She could not save him, did not save him. Her love could not save him. Harry cried and cried, grieving for the fragile little girl who adored him. She tried to hide the pain and shame under the covers, mortified and released in tandem. Sofia knew, Katia knew, and of course her mother knew. She never told another person. Harrison made an unconscious, unhealthy, twisted, self-sabotaging promise. Never hurt again. Now there was this beautiful boy lying beside her, not running. Zack peeled back the duvet, staring at Harry a long while with the kindest, most compassionate hazel eyes like her father. He caressed her cheek without saying one word. For the first time, she let go. She put all her faith in him. She believed he could save her, and he would. Zack loved the imperfect perfect she hid behind. Adelaide's mother and father choose not to give the past power, they lived each day. Their beach bubble existence was exquisite, even her mother's death would not diminish their love.

Adelaide knew the risks, having children. She was in love, pregnant and blissfully happy. She was a child of the sea, she trusted the currents, not the past. There was no time concept; in the ocean she was buoyant. Her father told her after Harry passed. It was too late for a moral compass; she already had her four little precious humans. Harry figured why hand her daughter a loaded Beretta? She was happy, her family was good, the girls were spectacular and her mother was dying. That couldn't be helped. Addie worried most about Georgia, her fiery hailstorm. Trudy and Zelda were chill babies, independent teens and stable adults. One in four, she knew the odds. Didn't think about it, she was too busy raising her girls, being a wife, a daughter. Maine, the earth away from her ocean, so many years, changed her. A sliver of fear snuck in. She read the statistics online while Caden was at work. "Hogwash, we made it this far," brushing his wife off. It was the one subject they argued about. "Jesus Addie, they're fine."

Addie wondered where were her selfish prick parents. Left her alone. Where were they today, right here, right now, when she really needed them? She tried ignoring the ick feeling, evil circling, sage it away. Her bowels knew, when each baby was born. She was in it, whatever came she would be there. She refused the black clouds, like her parents. She lived, loving every day being their mother. All these years, she'd been lucky. Her babies were good.

Until now.

Until this day.

She was wrong about Georgia being the one in four. Thank the lord.

She'd been so wrong.

Creole Colors

Too young to remember her grandmother, Maxine had two distinct memories of Harrison. One olfactory, the other bright, color sensory. Harry's flaming hair backlit by a canary yellow sun and periwinkle sky. Bright, happy colors waving at her, splashing about, being goofy with her sisters. Maxine loved the ocean, but hated the way the gritty sand rubbed her skin, the sun scorched her alabaster skin. She didn't complain, they were having too much fun. She had her books, cooler complete with veggies, PBJ & sliced watermelon. Max's tiny head disappeared under Harry's floppy hat, two sarongs spread out in the shade, her personal space. She didn't mind being separated from the others; she liked it. Max was born odd, quirky, an old soul and practically independent. She required little maintenance, which both freaked her mother out and didn't. She was a good girl, and her little helper with the twins. Max dressed in white, creams, neutrals; she loved her grandmother's funny colors. When her sisters teased her about her bland, boring *uniform,* Harry shushed them. "I wore black. Only black, not grey, dark black and I was famous. Black worked for me, until it didn't," sticking out her tongue. "Bodhi Tree, you and me?"

Maxine jumped up and down, clapping her hands unable to contain her excitement. The Bodhi Tree was a mystical world lined with rows and rows of imaginative books covered in angels and fairies. Her grandmother explained she was refueling the tank, a spiritual tune-up. Max had to look way, way up, crook

Jacqueline Cioffa

her neck to see Harry when she spoke. Rainbow chimes and crystals danced on the ceiling shooting flecks of light caught in their spell. The stained glass windows cast streams of afternoon sunlight, a secret, mystic code. The chubby, calico cat brushed Maxine's leg, purring. She giggled, kneeling down to rub her fat belly. "Ivy-ness, you sweetie, sweetie poo, did you miss me?" Ivy was a stray the bookstore adopted, the beloved mascot, who got far too many belly rubs. She was a very spoiled kitty. Bells jingled whenever someone opened or closed the door. Enchanted, Max was sure her grandmother introduced her to a dreamlike world. The six year old big, blue eyes mesmerized by every shiny crystal, tiger eye stone, the humongous tree in the garden, red scuffed plank floors, torn posters of funning looking men hung on the walls, behind the counter, the goofy man dressed in plaid shirt and striped shorts, the books she could not yet read, touching their spines, her grandmother greeted like a star. She did not know who Harrison had been, she was the grandmother Max idolized. Her skin prickly, giddy, childlike excitement, the secret time she did not have to share. It was the aroma that got her, as her growing mind and time began to fade the fond memory. The particular, pungent odor remained, the direct olfactory pathway to her long dead cherished grandmother and the bookstore that transformed into a fantasy world of fun. The Bodhi Tree, like most magic, is temporary. Buddhists believe the Bodhi tree sacred, sitting under it in quiet contemplation leads to 'awareness' and 'enlightenment.' Maxine did not understand the big word concept, or that her grandmother knew she was dying. She trusted how clean, happy, good it made her feel. Six year olds don't need grandiose, complicated explanations. Closed doors now, a depressing, blaze building sits in its place. The impressive Sacred Fig with heart shaped leaves remains, proud and majestic keeper of spirit secrets, grandmother-granddaughter afternoon visits buried deep inside her roots.

Patchouli. Max keeps a bottle on her nightstand, applying two dabs before sleep hoping to visit Harry in her dreams.

Her grandmother dressed in black? *No way*. Harry's aura was a twirling whirlpool of clean, bright clouds in alternating color. Max saw her outlines of turquoise, green, red, orange and a yellow halo encircling Harry's head. The large pink aura visible when her grandmother was *in between*, extending further away from earth. Max did not understand what was happening, the death concept came later. Pink is rare on earth and appears temporarily, and only when Zack was in close proximity. Maxine was attracted to color and scents and magic, every hue, shade, the brighter the better because of her. Harry gifted her with her consuming, passionate, color filled life, even if Max was most comfortable dressed in white. She dreamt she would open a small shop with a blinding turquoise storefront and hot pink sign, Good Scents where anyone could find her. Fill it with books, aroma and sparkles where wonders would be waiting, a fantastical garden with eucalyptus benches, comfy, cheery cushions, bamboo trees with flickering white lights, where day effortlessly met night. No clocks on the walls, time obsolete. She would serve healthy snacks, the basics, veggie sandwiches, fresh juices and herbal teas. Welcoming *all* people, Maxine would turn no person away. She believed everyone had pretty inside, born good. Some never knew magic; a Harry wasn't there to show them. She would change that, one little girl and calico cat *(well, maybe a puppy)* at a time. Maybe an awkward, lonely girl who took refuge in books would visit. A peculiar, quiet one much like herself with an unique name, might pop in. Maybe, Opal delicious. At Good Scents, strange and beautiful things happen, and are encouraged.

She finally found *her* place. A run down, in need of some major lovin' Creole Townhouse bordering the French Quarter. She waited, prayed and dare hoped, six was eons ago. Jake was coming, to design the garden, Georgia too. Max was deliriously happy. She could not believe her good fortune, most people never get the chance. The envelope, Harry did this. She knew it. Maxine was home, her patchouli dream built brick by brick with mortar.

Sugar Sugar

Georgia was late. Jake would be outside, honking the horn, annoyed. Frantically opening drawers, throwing clothes on the bed, running back and forth, bathroom toothpaste, toothbrush, shampoo. Shit, slow down girl. She could buy what she forgot and Max would have doubles. Max bought doubles of everything, drove her bonkers. She dumped the messy pile into the green duffle, threw on jeans, a v-neck, boots. Double-checking her purse, credit cards, driver's license, cash. All good. Jake despised airports, crowds, security, all the annoying shit that came before actually boarding a stinky, packed plane full of obnoxious overweight, rude passengers. He agreed to come, to help Max on one condition. They were driving. Georgia thought it over for less than two seconds, *duh*. Days and days alone with him in his truck, she was rose quartz and peacock pyrite happy. Yeah they spent all their time together, working. Sorting out Harry's Digs problems, logistics, orders, planning more efficient gardens. His face stuck in that stupid notepad, she was practically invisible. Georgia got him to agree to *bucket list* stops. Places en route that didn't deviate way off course from his very complex, detailed map. Jake was stiff, structured, boring, she wondered why she cared. Her cell rang. Georgia let it go to voice mail. Again, ringing from the kitchen. Twisting her hair, she bee-lined to silence the annoyance. Probably Jake, letting her know he was outside. She dug through her very overstuffed purse, throwing her house keys, wallet, make-up bag on the counter.

Ha, found the fucker, entered her passcode checking recent calls. Unknown, same number five times. It was her personal cell, only her mom, sisters, Jake and one other person had it. Georgia felt nauseated, the icky dread feeling you get when something very bad may be waiting at the other end of a call. Dial the goddamn number. A car horn beeped, Jake. Georgia ran to the screen porch, iPhone in hand, waving him off. He knew what every Georgia wave, mannerism meant. This wave was serious. Jake turned the keys and went to the porch. He sat in the rocker and waited. He knew better than to talk, the firestorm pacing back and forth might rip him apart.

"Okay, I understand. No, today, right this second. I'm leaving. Now. Wait."

Georgia collapsed, sobbing on the distressed plank floors, curled into fetal position. Jake stood, slowly, gently sat beside her. He'd never seen Georgia vulnerable, broken. Addie warned Jake, explained how bad it got after Zack. Asked if he'd check in when they left. She didn't eat, bathe for months. Pitiful babe wrapped in pops' sweater on the couch, shades drawn. By the time Jake stopped, a radiant Georgia was on the beach, board in the sand. She was smiling and chatting with kids. He never told her, she would've been pissed. Even worse, mortified. He loved her, he'd never tell. He made a promise to look after her. Funny, he couldn't stand to look at her, afraid she'd see him.

"Georgia, you're scaring me. Who's waiting? GODDAMN," Jake yelled, motionless. This was not the headstrong, infuriating girl he knew.

Georgia sat up, wiping snot on her t-shirt. She reached for a strand of hair, Jake grabbed her wrist holding firm. He had a millisecond to break the trance. He knew it was bad, she needed to be somewhere fast. He also knew the trip could wait, she wasn't going alone.

"Address? I'll drive." Jake wiped her face with his rough, strong hands, reaching under her armpits he pulled her up.

Georgia held onto Jake, everything was happening fast around her, not to her. Numb, she was numb. Numb, and ill.

"Long Beach. Long Beach Memorial."

Jake held Georgia's forearms firm, looking straight into her eyes with the reassurance she needed. "Okay, then. Get in the truck, I'll get your bag." Georgia did not argue; she took direction. Jake knew it was Miss Barbara, diabetes. She had had her leg amputated last month. Georgia visited her every day, brought fresh flowers, fixed healthy meals, took care of Jax. She was doing great, he didn't get it. Georgia never would have left her. She rested her head against the cold window, disappearing inside the glass.

Jake took short cuts, back roads, avoiding the freeway and congested morning commute. He'd made reservations near Arches National Park and Sante Fe to surprise her. Asked clients for recommendations, "eat at the Shed in Sante Fe, don't miss Chaco Canyon." He'd never left the nursery, LA, hell the state of California. Jake was excited to surprise her, super stoked for the adventure. Peeking at Georgia in fetal position, he forgot about the trip. He'd better call the office, cancel the reservations. Georgia insisted he use the corporate card, Maxine was *paying* him. She knew her sister, there were hundreds of awesome landscape architects in New Orleans. None of them understood the Good Scents concept, the garden vibe. *Bullshit,* she wanted Georgia, needed her close, did the conniving, well-played, smart thing. She called Jake. Little shit. Georgia loved Max but mostly she wanted to wring her scrawny, delicate neck. She didn't, Max needed her. Since she was born, Georgia was her protector, challenger, worst enemy, sister and second mother. Some things are without explanation. She and Max just are. Georgia rolled down the window, sticking her head out as far as possible. Her eyes shut from the force of the wind, equally violent and liberating.

"What are you, nuts? Get in here. Now." Jake yelled at the lunatic with half her extremities in his truck, the other half way out.

"Air." Georgia whispered, safely back in the cab. Arms crossed, upside down, disheveled carnival ride hair, cheeks rubicund. She looked like a pouty, ten year old seconds before an ugly cry, full out tantrum. She wouldn't, there was no time. In ten minutes, a frazzled, middle-aged woman dressed in a thrift store, lavender seersucker suit and cream color orthotics, waited. To deliver papers, a diaper bag purchased and packed by her. And one sniffling, frightened, missed his nap, overtired baby boy.

Boy 'O Boy

Before Jake found a spot, Georgia grabbed her purse, opened the door and sprinted. Halfway inside the door she turned and shouted, "Lobby, meet us."

Us. He circled, spotting a dude in a sleeveless Dogstown t-shirt, shredded jeans and full leg cast hobbling on crutches. A young, pretty, gangly chick in a white muscle tee and black leather vest juggling helmets ran to the passenger side. Dude was lucky, this time. Hurry up goddamn bikers. Jake shot a half nod when they pulled out.

Jake quickly scanned the signs, Lab, X-Rays, Registration, Gift Shop, no lobby. Where was the damn lobby? Gurneys, nurses' aides, doctors in scrubs flew past. An elderly man with an oxygen tube in his nose and walking stick sat next to an Hispanic teenager with black fingernails and a round belly. She fidgeted in her chair, uncomfortable, biting her polish. A toddler sat on the floor between her chubby ankles, playing with wood blocks. Wow, the halls were jammed for a Tuesday morning. All of Compty was there. Then he remembered, the county hospital closed, budget cuts. It was the only Community Hospital that accepted Medicaid, VA Vets, addicts, criminals, mentally unstable, elderly and the poor. Shit man, this country has gone to hell.

"Excuse me, do you know where the lobby is?" Jake asked the pregnant girl, she shook her head. The old guy sat up happy to help. "Which?" He was a lifer, heart disease, knew every floor, nurse and hotshot doctor. Think, Jake. "My friend, diabetes, leg amputee, not good." The silver fox's face got serious, reached for Jake's forearm, patting it the way you comfort a sick dog.

"Miss Barbara?" Jake nodded.

"I'm sorry son, she's gone." I know that, dickhead. What floor???!!!

"What floor," politely removing his silver fox hand.

"She won't be there, she'll be in the morgue. I recognized a pretty gal with red hair fly through the lobby. Is she yours?" pointing towards the elevator bank.

Jake nodded, trying to keep cool. "She's her daughter," not sure why he lied. "Four. There's a small room for families," silver fox scrunched his forehead, perplexed. Miss Barbara was black and the gal, white. He missed his wife, the routine, going to work and coming home to a warm plate, 6:00 o'clock on the dot. Life was simpler, everything was moving too fast for him. He liked Miss Barbara, she talked to him in physical therapy and nobody talked. Made him laugh. That girl was lucky, today not so much. "Thank you sir," Jake shouted halfway down the hall. He didn't bother with the elevator, taking the stairs two at a time.

The stale, mint green halls smelled of death, sickness and sadness. Jake did not get why they didn't paint the walls a more cheerful color. Jesus, he'd rather shovel shit then catch something, wind up in the ER. This was the second time he'd been inside since he was seven. Busted foot, skateboard present. His ankle throbbed as he scoured the halls looking for her. Fogged windows, curtains drawn, door closed, Jake took a minute. He stood outside the door, adjusted his shirt, hair and caught his breath. He knocked softly, and waited. Again. A portly, "kindly nurse" opened the door.

Jax was sound asleep on the carpet, sandwiched by his blankie. Thumb in his mouth, blue teddy in the crook of his arm. Georgia's back to him, she sat in a plastic chair, the table covered in a white cloud of papers, and next to her sat some scrawny, tired-looking woman who kept checking time on her phone. Nurse Burly whispered in Georgia's ear, she nodded and motioned, razor-focused on the paper in her hand. Jake rested his hand on her shoulder, letting her know he was there. She nodded without looking, didn't dare. Her friend was dead, she couldn't cry or mourn. The annoyed, matter-of- fact, pretend to give a shit social worker talked. Georgia saw her lips moving, unable to process. She used big words, legal jargon Georgia didn't understand. Tucker, her lawyer, shit, she meant "el Stinko," should be here.

"Lady, slow down. English," Georgia comforted a whaling baby on the back, two pats, three circles, two pats, three circles. Jax's limbs relaxed, his breathing calmed in her arms. Georgia rummaged through the diaper bag, grabbing a blanket. She spread it out, knelt down, gently placing him to one side and swaddling him with the remainder. She waited, holding her breath. A tear rolled off her cheek, she couldn't go there. Apparently Miss Barbara knew what she was doing. She knew, the first time she placed Jax on her lap.

"I'm all they got," Miss Barbara wasn't dramatizing. She was stating a fact.

Georgia's head hurt, fingers cramped. She must have signed her name fifty times. In proper legal language, Miss Barbara had named her Jax's temporary guardian. "A formality," sear-sucker explained. *If* she wanted him. If not, no problem, he went into the system. *No problem*, fat shit. No one would contest, his mother had given up parental rights. "The brothers?" Georgia peeked at Jax with sadness, terror, love and remorse. The boys will live with an aunt. She worked two jobs, had grown children, grandbabies, no way was she taking a baby. NO infant. Miss Barbara called when they took her leg, she could smell the decay. She knew she wasn't going home, never would leave that hospital. She was okay with it, dying, right with God. She prayed hard over Georgia. Before she drifted into the white nothingness, disappeared inside a mess of plastic tubes, machines and the hose shoved down her throat, she thought of the boy. Miss Barbara knew in her heart Jax was already Georgia's the minute she saw their eyes lock. A redheaded, spitfire, white chick with the pure heart and a chocolate milkshake delicious baby boy the perfect match. She stopped trying to second- guess what God was thinking ages ago. Miss Barbara could not save her son with her love and prayers, her one regret. She'd gladly trade her life for her son's, that she would do willingly. Pink lemonade, lightning force in camouflage, tool belt slung around her waist walking towards her, smiling, Jax cooing behind. It was the last image Miss Barbara saw before her heart quit. It was a good, honest life. Georgia was honest, and good.

The aunt said, bring the boy round anytime.

Georgia picked up the pen, looked at the helpless creature snug in his blanket. She wondered, petrified what he would think of her in twenty years when he was a smart-ass punk who hated her guts. She thought of all the countless scenarios, ways she would fuck up his life, started to sweat. One more signature. She spun around searching for Jake, shock on her face, twisting a strand of hair. He was sitting on the musty, scratchy couch where'd he'd been the whole time. Georgia let out a sigh when she found him. Jake nodded, once. One time was all she needed. The social worker shook her hand, straightened the paperwork stuffing it into the overstuffed sack. She adjusted the crease in her pant leg, soft shook Jake's hand and made a beeline for the door.

"Someone will be in touch, home visit. Formality, don't worry dear." Georgia's violet face matched her hair, two seconds away from airborne. Paralyzed, stuck, her legs betrayed her; she wanted to get up and kill the bitch. Jake went to her, pulled out a pint-size plastic chair, and waited. Hotheaded, no bother talking to Georgia while she was in Georgia tilt-a-whirl. She'd spin out eventually, done processing.

"Jake?" Georgia spoke softly.

"Yup." Not real sure she was all the way back.

"What just happened?" Georgia looked thirteen, around the age they first met.

He wanted to wrap his arms around her, comfort her. That's the last thing she needed, hated the mush.

"I saw a Costco, ten minutes tops. You two okay?" She needed a car seat, diapers, hell if he knew. He'd ask. Georgia smiled, a Jake smile reserved for him.

"Sorry."

"For…?" Jake knew, vacation. "Are you kidding? Two weeks of no compost, no community garden, no broken irrigation systems, no nursery, no heavy lifting."

"Stop, it's not funny." Georgia giggled, thanking God for dependable, gorgeous, solid, not easily rattled Jake. He was her business partner, green thumb mentor, forever friend and home away from home person. Shit, Max.

"I'll call Maxine," reading her face. "We could fly, bring him. You're always nagging, you're ripe for adventure."

"Really?" Georgia wanted to cry, she was exhausted.

"What the hell," shrugging it off in the nonchalant way only Jake could. He winked halfway out the door tipping his imaginary cowboy hat, "two shakes."

One-Trick Pony

Jake returned to the hospital with a pimped out, BOB Revolution all-terrain, orange and black utility stroller. Georgia was on the couch holding a cooing, happy baby. He was taking a bottle, holding a strand of hair with his tiny fingers smiling at her. Thank heaven he was a chill baby, Georgia could only handle one thing at a time. He dealt with the business side; she handled the creative. They made a good team. *This*, this was not green vegetable, red tomato fruit, gardenia, magnolia, Georgia Pine garden comfort. The boy was Mars, Pluto, Venus unqualified, extra terrestrial out there territory. Jake found a pretty, petite lady that screamed mom at Costco. He was spot on, high fivers. Jake walked out with a trifold receipt, a variety of baby paraphernalia so Georgia would never have to leave the Cove. The back of the truck was fully loaded. She rolled her eyes at the rugged, disgustingly handsome, muscular, jeans and t-shirt every-man, pushing a very loud, orange stroller, and preceded to get the stupid giggles, the crazy, teary cannot stop, ridiculously cathartic kind. Jake brought in his already packed, army duffle. "Where should?" pointing to the hall.

"Take Zack's, on the left," Georgia motioned, the knot in her neck loosening. She hadn't felt this kind of fear or dread since high school. The fire building in her gut destructive, the overwhelming need to run. A hostage in her own life even if it wasn't true. She was spiraling, until she looked down. Sparkle baby was propped in the middle of the kitchen floor, content, beating metal pans with a wooden spoon. Ouch, eardrum. He was such a good boy, jovial and independent. Self-pity sprinkled with a dose of guilt stopped the tilt-a-whirl long enough to send Georgia flying. She was grounded by the cool porcelain tile and off-beat drummer. And Jake was staying, there was *that*.

"Maybe you'll stop bragging and break out those boards. The ones I hear about, non-stop," Jake shouted from Zack's room. He felt weird, icky being there, in that house, sleeping in his room. Zack wouldn't mind, he was taking care of *her* as promised. He found swim shorts, changed his shirt and slipped on brown leather Birks. Jake had never taken a vacation, a day off, hell, he deserved this. No twenty pound munchkin, or Georgia moody was going to ruin his fourteen-day pass.

They looked liked a lopsided, topsy-turvy family, descending the rocky steps, Georgia hauling a messenger bag across her chest, Jax on her back waving at an overloaded Jake. Juggling a nylon cooler, diaper bag, beach pack and long board, he could've made two trips. He didn't want to miss out. Why this place, how an afternoon in the sea, napping in the shade to the sound of waves, was way better than any sound machine. No wonder she never left. Georgia's Cove was exactly how she described it, but way better. His shoulders relaxed, back ached less, jaw loosened, he imagined a young Zack, virile, tan knees, propped elbows, hugging them.

Jax's mouth opened wide when the frigid surf tickled his teeny toes. Georgia was uncharacteristically patient, dangling over him to catch a reaction. Before Jake reached for the sunscreen, she had Jax on his belly riding the waves, the sun's reflection off the water shadow dancing between them. They were crazy happy, the enormous board devouring the baby. She was in her world, waves calm and Jax cheery. He could not hear them but he saw Jax giggling for the first time in days. Georgia looked exactly like Zack when she smiled. Why he hadn't noticed the resemblance before he knew without asking. Georgia was probably born with tiny fists in pugilistic stance, while Zack's were wide open. The soft edges she inherited from Zack, osmosis ripples. She was good earth, soil bountiful and ripe. Jake discovered he craved a little lopsided. She was damn right, per Georgia Pine fashion. The Cove was something kind of exceptional and a whole lot of magic. He was in love with the infuriating, capable, stubborn, fierce, loyal, crimson pyre and brimstone woman.

Jake was spellbound by the jagged midnight granite, quartz granules, by the beach where the bluff and rough terrain meet the harmonious, long-winded ocean and keeper of secrets. The modest house on a hill is in need of a paint job, gardens abundant, flora freedom with each inhale. This is the private sanctuary Georgia's grandparents cured and cultivated with love. Adoration so deep, it permeated the skin with memory. Watching her wade through the ocean, the waves lapping her tan torso, blissfully unaware, Jake felt like a bandit. The statuesque, crimson goddess moved effortlessly in her world. The afternoon sun's tidal reflection beamed turquoise pools illuminating Georgia, as she tossed Jax high into the air. Neither recognized the past repeating. Adelaide would, Harrison would, Zack, the quiet observer, definitely would. They lived the same mystical, irreplaceable, unrepeatable scene. Georgia could not explain the déjà-vu living under her skin, shake Harrison's omnipresence, nor deny it. Harry's flashbulb existence, the lingering spirit coiled and tangled her blood and veins. The encapsulating, ferocious, brave, safe, invisible connection. Only now with the weight of the precious, jovial *new-new* creature's future in Georgia's outstretched arms, did she understand. Generational, gestational, unconditional, forever bound, limitless, elusive, custodial, infinite, weight bearing, ferocious Mother-love.

Ananta

Dear you-know-who, I want to forgive you. To do better, feel a whole lot better. I want to be enlightened in sleep so I might wake better, filled with less waste, hate and rage. How can I envision ethereal moral characters, women of strength, women of character, messy, multifaceted women, vulnerable, chaotic women who don't hide flaws behind shame; they celebrate them. Women ruled by love, and decent, confident men worthy of their affections. I don't get it, this lunchbox life isn't working. I've wasted so many hours stuck, believing one moment defined me. There must be more than this unbearable terror, numbing pain and hollow body. I am nothing, infinite tumbleweed on desert plains without these characters. They make me better. They make me whole.

Opal (Seven) exists in the real world with a fifty-fifty death sentence. A postcard from Big Sur says it's so, inscribed with three words, "YOU did this." That should be enough, puff the chest proud, all the blasé adjectives the unimaginative writer uses, lazy forms of self-expression. It's not, laughable at best. The absent sun plays tricks on the memory, woods blanketed by fear, days feel the same, uniformly gray, while the sun's light shines on a different longitude. Happy remains far, far away and forever foreign. X remembers her mother, the trails, how the gravel crunched underfoot, pussy willows and horsetail higher than her four-year-old imagination. Her mom at her side, X believed the woods made them strong, together invincible. Baby chipmunks scurried past, doe's eyes smiled at her, funny lavender flowers scattered along the walk, sunny buttercups, (that's what X called them) yellowed her chin. Neon blue and green Nikes played catch-up with light spots. Unafraid, the high priestess roamed magical gardens. Fear came, fell from the rain gutters, dirty drops, distant thunder, awkward silence no one else heard, ridiculous homemade misconceptions. She wondered how she got here, this moment, a world without sun. X spent life existing, red, velvet cloaked in the safety of the familiar, gray zone, ugly and disfigured. Misdirected, mad at the wrong persons, mother, nurse, brother, cruel kids on the block, doctors, hell even the too skinny, too tan, too rich, 'look at me,' too entitled celebrity on television. Anger is a secondary emotion, what comes first? The five year old crushed, sliced and diced child cannot grasp the benefits of therapeutic license. Why, why the hell not? The bitter, pissed, most hatred hurled in heaven's direction. Half a human with whole emotions, what the hell was she doing here? Tell me, you tell me. X forgot, she stopped believing in fairy tales. Trust the characters, the humanistic stories dissected, her story, this story, your story tossed together in the salad spinner. She's working through shit, one tangled, twisted sentence at a time. Transference. Big word, an extensive vocabulary came easy to the kid ricocheting between chair and sterile bed.

X prays, in spite of her agnostic, angry self, before turning out the lights, backing up and powering down her laptop. Maybe, slim shot sunshine is better than no shot if she gets the story right. Maybe, the boogeyman hiding in her woods, lurking behind every tree, twig snap and wind brush will leave her, for good.

Astropop

Georgia could not stop staring at her sister. Lounging in Good Scents Max's recently completed, beyond belief, beauteous garden, Jake surpassed his landscaping ability. The meticulous blueprints, her sister's transcendent, ethereal impossible vision. Teak wood benches formed a U, plush charcoal-brown cushions, burnt-orange pillows and throws looked organic, and inviting. Georgia argued it was too fancy for a store. Max shook her head whispering, "you'll see." Ten foot giant running bamboo planters lined the walls, blue-white lights hung from the wooden slats on the ceiling. Sea foam, turquoise and yellow beach glass chandeliers collected by a little girl over summer breaks at the Cove, danced and dazzled above. It was the second most stunning place she'd ever seen. Max had recreated her intimate, fairy tale rendition of the Cove. Georgia's hazel eyes beaming, ginger waves worn loose and long, skin glowing, mouth turned slightly upward told Max everything. Georgia's was the only reinforcement she craved. Jax stirred, scrunching his nose against the cushion. Georgia swiftly adjusted the throw removing it from his chubby cheeks, stroking his back. Jax settled, Georgia looked at Max shrugging her shoulders. Maxine nodded, Georgia had been mothering her since she was born. Maxine wanted to quiet her most of the time, she was infuriating, stubborn and exasperating. She missed her most when she was gone. Georgia pushed Max to live outside the insulated world in her head, pushed her to do things she wouldn't dare on her own. She was always right,

Maxine *could* dream bigger, go farther, be more without coming apart. Georgia did not treat Max like the others, babied enough by her family. Adelaide called Georgia crying, "she can't do this. It's too much."

"Jesus Christ mom, too much for her or for you?" Georgia realized there was a good chance her mom might be right, fuck it. She knew Max. This was it, her one dream since she was seven. She'd keep her up at night describing the store, exactly how it would look, the colors on the walls, who would come, down to the books on the shelves. Georgia would put the pillow overhead and scream, kicking her feet against the sheets begging her to shut up. Here they were, grownups, adults with full lives and she could not stop staring at her transparent, pure, radiant, lovely sister. The one who traded her prized gooey, three-stripe delicious Astropop for a plain old black rock with diamond veins. Georgia snickered, only allowed candy on special occasions, birthdays and Christmas. She looked at the wall above Max's head, in a carved nook sat the rock floodlit by a single halo. It was magnificent, silver veins throwing streaks of light complimenting the shimmering midnight-black stone. Georgia couldn't see potential when they were kids, all she saw was a stupid old rock. Max knew. Even as a child, she found beauty extraordinary in the ordinary.

Max spotted an aluminum, rusty shack held together by duct tape on one Saturday afternoon flea market drive. An old man with silver hair and no teeth sat on a crate carving intricate designs in salvaged wood. Sweat beads of labor fell from his forehead, interrupting the work. Annoyed he stopped to wipe them with a dirty, torn hankie from his back pocket. Maxine pulled over in her vintage, robin's egg blue Chevy pickup.

"Sir, excuse me sir."

"Speak your words, child. Louder." He had lost everything when the levies busted. His home, health, dignity, pride. His wife up and left after a time, went South to her sister's. This plot was his, his birthright, shotgun house home, he wasn't budging. The spirits wouldn't find him come time, and his heartbeat was slowin.' FEMA wanted to relocate, move the whole neighborhood into tin boxes. Then what? Some took the dough, damn fools. Forced to come back to nothin', no job, money, collecting cans to pay the electric. Government wanted those tin cans back, kicking them like feral cats. He served his country, got a license, fixed the small house, knew about hard work. Stubborn old jester, they whispered. He ignored the talk, welcomed the whodi back. If he had to live in a shack, damn well be his own, on land bought by his grand pappy. He lived in the shed, no water, no toilet, walked five miles twice a week to wash. A white plastic bucket with the missing handle held his toothbrush, soap, washcloth and towel. Sold furniture to buy bread, water, eggs, in a good week roast chicken. Shameless, greed filled bastards; white men in suits. Maxine felt the tears choke in her throat, she did not dare disrespect him with waterworks. She opened her purse, reached for her checkbook.

"I need a unique, custom table with book slots, twenty by twenty for my store, the garden outback. Some benches, ottomans too. If I buy the wood, can you help with the design? Who should I write the deposit to?"

"M-e-t-t-u-s, T-h-a-d-d-e-u-s. Everyone calls me M.T.. Hold up, I didn't start yet. Lady, what if I take off with the dough."

"Well, M.T. you just told me you'll never leave your land. I'm confident you won't. Besides, I'm new, I could really use your expertise, someone with deep roots. Come by the store next week, you'll see. I'll pick you up." Maxine gently placed the check on the driftwood, stood up and headed to the pickup. "Mr. Mettus, don't let the bastards run you down. Saturday."

M.T. frowns, not quite sure who the white windstorm was. His mother had the gift for reading people, some say she was a witch. Raised in a mercurial house where spirits were welcome, sage burned and calendar days set by the sun and linear moon cycles. He wasn't afraid of the lady, good vibe. He reached down to turn over the check: $5,000.00, lagniappe, lady is *crazy*.

Georgia ran her fingers over the intricate design groove etchings in the wood. Lotus flower, fleur-de-lis, crescent moon, stars and circular mazes. There was nothing tacky, ornate, or overdone, each piece masterly carved with NEW AWR-LINZ magic and love. The celebratory bottle of Kirkland Brut Rose, two flutes of pink bubbles sat directly in front of the sisters. Dixie beer bottles, 'Blackened Voodoo,' lined the far edge of the table where Jake sat dozing.

Georgia promised Maxine she would stay for the opening, they'd been there almost a month.

Harry's Digs, home visits, adoption process to get back to, she almost wished she could stay. She was intoxicated by the city, row houses, French architecture. Jax loved the butterflies at Audubon Park, Carousel Gardens. She and Jake indulged in late evening po-boy sandwiches and local beer sampling. Georgia loved the eclectic flavor, 'Second Linin,' hated the drunk tourists, redneck crowds. When she discovered the haunting Spanish moss dripping from massive cypress trees, rundown stately manors and mysterious, slow moving, swamp waters of the Bayou, she shared Max's childhood fascination with the deep South, promised to return. Old charm Voodoo mystery co-exists with plastic, garish multi-color beads and new world tradition in harmony. Yes, Maxine got it.

Max cried and cried, begging Georgia not to go. Full on, two-year-old meltdown outside Good Scents, three carry-ons, stroller, messenger bags and two strapping men, one tall, tan, muscular and handsome, the other roly-poly delicious, half-naked, chocolate on her hip.

"You done good," lifting her sister's chin, calming her like she would Jax. "Mom and daddy are coming; you've got Mettus. You're being ridiculous," Georgia snapped, big sister mode.

A navy blue Carriage Company SUV showed up right on time to take Georgia, Jake and Jax to the airport. Max looked pitiful as she gripped the car window. Georgia hated this part; she had to go. Prying Max's fingers from the glass one by one, she spoke slow and deliberately. "The Cove is your home. Come back, no questions. Check the garden, we left something."

Pants On, Pants Off

Max nodded her head back and forth the way a child does, listening intently, placing their trust in the adult speaking. As if they had the answers, *as if*. Georgia uncurled her baby sister's pinky, peeked at Jax asleep sucking his fist. Georgia tried not to cry; it wasn't like she'd never see her again. She let one tear escape, began twisting a strand of hair. Oh boy, Jake reached over the car seat for her hand. Squeezing tight.

Maxine ran to the garden throwing herself onto a bench, sobbing into a pillow. She cried and cried, her heart shattered beach glass in too many pieces. She wasn't even sure why she was crying, over emotional her mom would say. If she was there, she'd stroke her hair, hum, stay with her. Max was her sweet, sensitive, peculiar child who never quite became a grown up. Adelaide worried a little more, fussed a little more, protected her a little more and loved her as much as she needed.

Maxine woke disoriented, to purple and pink clouds floating past the skylight. The dusk hour, the spirit guides favorite time to visit. She sat up, wrapped the throw around her shoulders, wiping sleep from her eyes. Harry. Her grandmother was there, she could feel her, she hadn't visited in so long.

Harrison sat behind her granddaughter, taking in the peace, serenity and beauty of the garden. She wanted to gasp, to be alive in human form, to hold Maxine in her arms. She had no idea the child was paying attention, the weekly excursions to the bookstore meant to be a distraction, fun. Harrison concentrated hard, focusing all her energy towards the Bodhi tree, rattling the leaves with a steady gust of wind.

Max hadn't noticed the tree. Georgia and Jake snuck it in when she went to bed. The tears started, not weepy but the incredulous, overwhelming kind. The sacred tree represented everything Harry had shown her, meant to distract the impressionable, painfully different, timid grandchild. The Bodhi Tree, *multi-layered, rich, complex symbol of the self and its journey towards enlightenment.* Maxine didn't ask what the big words meant; she had felt them since birth, and beyond. In awe of her ever changing, aura swirl, radiant grandmother she'd follow her anywhere.

Harrison knew things, benefits of the dead. She had to see Max, once. What a striking, rare beauty. More generous, kind, compassionate than most. Oh Maxine, what have you done? In utero, we map out our blueprints meticulously. With the first gasp for oxygen, glimpse of shadows and light, being held in a mother's warm, capable arms we become imperfectly perfect. No longer free to alter the plans. Harry believed she could change hers with stubborn will, brute force. Idiotic waste of energy, she knew better. Why child, didn't you choose an alternate route? Harrison's no longer beating heart hurt, heavy. Why didn't you pick the easier path? You, of course, Maxine of maddening faith, never would.

Max closed her eyes and took a long, restorative healing breath sniffing jasmine and sweet magnolia. She envisioned a bountiful, ripe fig tree and charming, cobblestone, antique village in Italy. Intimate details of Harrison's life, Max would remember. Good Scents.

Harrison was with her, in her fairy-tale garden of lights off the French Quartier, where great spirits and voudon magic wander aged streets and centuries old oak trees. She felt less alone, at home with her lonesomeness. Since as far back as she could remember, Max never envisioned a future. It didn't bother

her, frighten her, her future was a never-ending transparent, squishy, bouncy ball of white with the tiny speck (*she presumed her*) in the middle. The speck never grew or changed dimension while the ball got small and smaller.

This white circumference felt less like dread than any space she'd known. Harry was gone. Max took off her Tom's, stretched out pulling the blanket snug and drifted without dreaming. Mettus peaked in, dimmed the lights and double-checked the chain lock on the back door.

Wee House

Two semi's parked in front of Mettus' decrepit plot with a crew, lumber, furniture and mini appliances. In eighteen days he had a brand new tiny house complete with bed, kitchen, bathroom, running water, electricity on wheels. Maxine didn't ask, she did what needed to be done. If she didn't spend Harry's fortune on others, what kind of person was she? She had her Creole townhouse, funky, modern loft above her dream shop, enough clothes, shoes, accessories and food with millions leftover in her trust. It was hilarious, Max could take exotic vacations, five star resorts, buy posh property in Hollywood next to the stars, she had the means. Her trust quadrupled over the years, thanks to careful investing by Tucker. Not even a Porsche, silly sport cars, Max bought a Prius with a sunroof instead. She preferred her truck; maybe Mettus would swap. She helped, because she should. It made her feel good.

Mettus showed up outside the store, in khakis and ironed work shirt. Took him three hours and five buses to get there. No words, just a nod.

You and I and You

Max paid M.T. a generous wage, helped him apply for health insurance and told him he was free to come and go. Help out when he was up to it. He came every day, mopped floors, unpacked boxes, stocked books, cleaned the bathroom, polished the antique register, dusted shelves. Basically, anything. They shared meals in the garden. A hanky dabbing, one hundred degree Louisiana night, Mettus kept fidgeting under the table. Wincing under breath with every movement. Max dropped her fork, stood and went into the shop, grabbing her keys off the hook behind the register.

"License valid?"

"No, ma'am." Mettus shook his head in shame, staring at his plate.

"Heads up," tossing keys in his direction. "Details, we'll sort it out. Take the truck. Blisters, don't want you walking."

"Yes, ma'am."

"Max. Maxine works too," winking.

Harrison worried when she set up the trusts she wouldn't be there to advise her granddaughters. Girls *never* listened to their mothers; Adelaide was screwed. They were doing fine with that kind of money, better than fine. Harry guessed Max might gift some, forever collecting broken birds, toads, dead fish for Zack, tears flooding her glassy, blue eyes. She wanted to save them.

"Fix him, pretty please." Zack would stroke her back, trying to explain he couldn't.

Inconsolable, incomprehensible ten-year-old tears, "you're Dr. Pretty, you have to." Zack kissed the top of her forehead and flat out lied. He told her he'd take it to the hospital. Max's *perma* worry expression melted, she skipped off in search of the next rescue. The dumpster at the top of the hill was Zack's operating room of choice. He always said a little prayer before tossing the critter, usually the lyrics from a tune playing on the radio.

Maxine never gave Harry's money much thought. Except, she was a very, very, very lucky person. She planned to spend it, to keep spending. Her rescue's more vital than a petite, blond, sea urchin's good intention. No matter how far the *adult* heart strays, you never escape the beginnings.

Good Scents was doing so well, Maxine hardly had time to Skype. A few months after opening, a dozen editors asked for interviews, *Elle Décor, Homes and Garden, NY Magazine, O Magazine* and a bunch of others she needed to Google. The store wasn't the whole story, the lady white, Hollywood royalty giving back was the hook. The bar was a hit; Max kept the menu basic. Roast beef po-boy, fried shrimp po-boy and an avocado, lettuce, and tomato for the occasional vegetarian, organic/ not organic French bread. She found a garden-fresh, novel neighborhood restaurant happy to cater the store. Drinks, water, honest-to-sweetness southern iced tea, with a lemon peel or sprig of mint, café au lait, and spice, ginger, currant, basil herbal teas served in mason jars. Mettus had a sixteen yr. old granddaughter, Eveleen. Already prettier than Halle Berry, lived down in Terre aux Boeufs with her mom, worked busing tables. Maxine hired her before they met, rented a small studio for her in walking distance to keep an eye out. Every dawn before opening, Mettus set up a plastic folding table on the sidewalk, with fifty free, freshly made sandwiches. Maxine peeked through the curtain, not wanting to scare anyone off. The neighborhood had lost so much they were right to be skeptical, held tight to their pride. Mothers came first, with scrawny, hungry kids taking *only* two sandwiches, never more than needed. Making sure the babies got fed. Then came the crack-heads, dealers, robbers and thieves. Max turned no one away. She didn't distinguish between good and evil, in her mind everyone was welcome.

This was what she dreamed, hoped, helping others. A store purchase was a plus. She wrote the same message on the chalkboard in pastel colors, 'Welcome. Good Scents is *your* store.' Two months, three months, six months, Max was there, stocking books, cleaning the garden, making café au lait. She was feeling her way, making a home. The locals began to trust the eccentric, flighty, odd white woman dressed in all-white, calling her *Bianca*. The word Bianca so special in female naming because it can mean fair-skinned and also means white. Reigning since 1983, Bianca is a widely loved and powerful voodoo queen in New Orleans. Maxine loved the nickname, spot on and soulful.

A&D Ointment

Jake watched Georgia stomp up and down the aisle, twisty, cranky baby in her arms. Slightly amused, he didn't dare look in her direction. Not even two hours away from her sister, Georgia was back in well, Georgia mode. Ginger waves of hair hung halfway down her back captivating, sing-songing back and forth with each pivot. Poor Jax. Georgia fumbled through her purse for her phone, scanning contacts unsuccessfully for the car service. Jax kept knocking her hand, picking up on Georgia's nervous energy. She squeezed squirmy baby's diaper, lifted him to smell his butt and thrusted him and the diaper bag in Jake's lap without warning. Plopping down defeated, frazzled in a vacant chair, she began absentmindedly twisting a strand of hair. "I can't."

Jake smiled, scoured the diaper bag for a binky and stuck it in Jax' mouth, kissing the top of his head, rubbing his belly. In thirty seconds, Jax settled, cooing and holding Jake's strong, calm hand. Georgia wanted to scream, brats. What was it? Why was she so upset? It wasn't Max, they'd lived their entire adult lives apart. That wasn't it. They Skyped, same as forever. She promised they'd come back, soon as the legal crap was straight. El Stinko was on it. Jake, damn it, she meant *Jax*. Was adopting an infant on her own freaking her the fuck out? Sure a little, it wasn't like she didn't have a full-on-support swat team. Her mother was driving her nuts, when can we visit? "The twins want to come, it'll be a reunion. Jax can meet his cousins!" Texts all day long, packages with baby paraphernalia. Even her dad went nuts, sent a drone and motorized mini fishing boat. He'd be ten before he could use them. What the hell were they thinking, why was she so goddamn pissed, infuriated. She took out her phone, looked up the car service, glanced at Jake and the super content, calm baby in his arms, pissed. *He* was her problem. He couldn't play daddy, partner, friend and disappear. Georgia had a child now and grown up responsibility. She had to stop pining, forget him. He was there, available. It was making her nuts. She couldn't do it; she couldn't stop. That's the screaming, two-year-old tantrum, infuriating emotions swimming in her gut. Jake, smiling, gorgeous, capable, loving, sweet, available Jake, was the most painful kind of ambiguous.

"One car or two?" Georgia held her mouth over the speaker.

Jake held up one finger. Georgia twisted a lock of hair even faster. Ambivalence, there it was again. She never wondered what Jake was thinking before. Jake was refreshing, honest, reliable Jake. The open, easy-going guy she'd known since she was a smart-ass, gawky teenager. What the hell was going on. Georgia pointed to the restrooms. Jake nodded. She really needed to get the hell out of there, splash cold water on her face. "Did you really think I'd take off?" Jake shouted after her. Georgia walked faster, dismissing him, pulling the front of her hair. To the passengers, it looked like a lover's quarrel, except Jake was smiling and Georgia was not. Mad? Georgia looked at her stunning face sans makeup, and sulking, sad eyes. His presence, and absence were breaking her heart. She'd tell him, no more mixed messages. She'd tell him to go home, his home. The Cove was her and Jax' home. She had to start behaving like a mother, take care of her son. Wow, her reflection in the glass went from sad to shock in three seconds. That was the first time she used the word, *son*. Scary as summer storms, Jake was not helping. Jake was thinking the same, watching Jax kick his tiny Nikes in the air, content to be in his lap. He'd tell her, scary as hell. This was the family he wanted. Her, the petulant child, teenage brat, stubborn woman he loved the moment she breezed into the nursery barking orders. To hell with Zack, he kept his promise long enough.

Garanimals

The car hadn't come to a stop up the winding drive, Georgia flung open the door, unbuckled the car seat, grabbed their suitcases and threw them on the lawn. Jake thanked the driver, left him a generous tip. His duffle was still in the trunk. Georgia turned from the porch, zonked Jax in tow, glaring in his direction, "Why are you still here?"

Slamming the screen porch, she headed for the nursery. Gently lifting dead weight, sleeping boy and placing him in his crib. Georgia bent down, brushed his forehead, and uncovered his feet. Just beginning to learn his rhythms, Jax had screamed the first time she tucked him in snug, kicking free his adorable feet. "You and me bud, we'll figure it out," Georgia whispered. She turned on the baby monitor, garanimals nightlight, paused in the doorway to watch him sleep. Satisfied Jax was in REM, she walked towards the unavoidable dread, rocking on the porch. Stopping at the barren fridge, a six pack of Hoegaarden looked lonely. Perfect, Jake *hates* Hoegaarden, says it's girlie beer. Ha, popping two bottles. Jake waits, listening to the ocean's sounds wondering how many creatures, pirates and sea dwellers of years past have been in his spot. The sun descending in the sky, the half-moon rising takes cover behind alternating violet and peach clouds. He wonders, is the moon in love with the sun, living for their transitory encounters, an agony he can agree with. The door slams, startling him. "I should fix that," speaking to Georgia's tense shoulders, and tight back.

Jacqueline Cioffa

"Don't even think about it," Georgia quips, annoyed. He doesn't know the story. She's standing above him holding out a beer. Jake takes it, gently grabbing her forearm. "Sit," spoken with authority; she's caught off guard. Georgia sits, setting the baby monitor on the table between them, a protective shield. "This, I can't…"

"Georgia, would you shut up, listen. For once." Jake takes a swig of his liquid courage, making a face. "I'm going to tell you a story, a fable since you've been acting like a two-year-old all week. Most of it you've heard. Never from me, my perspective." Jake sits at attention, twelve pack turns in her direction, facing Georgia Pine.

There was an introverted, awkward kid, worked at his family's nursery after school. He didn't want to, he wanted to play lacrosse. Lacrosse was his world, scouts recruited him to play college, full scholarship. Free ride. His mother cried, said she was sorry. Life was hard, best he learned now. Tradition, that's what loyal sons do. He wanted to break something, rebel, wasn't brave like his father. He didn't even *like* flowers, vegetables, compost. Gardening was for sissies, girls. Until a Santa Ana gust of wind blew through the gardens. The boy almost fell over from the force. He looked towards the door. It wasn't a wind gust, it was a young girl holding some man's hand. The boy was too busy gawking at the girl to look at the guy. He knew him, Zack. Nice fella, came in for years with his knockout wife. Harrison was a famous actress, who was cool. It kinda grossed him out, the kisses, hand holding. He was a teenager, what the hell did he know. They tipped well. Zack didn't come in for many, many years. He heard the lady died; too bad, she was nice. The girl. There was something familiar, not *friend* familiar. Eye contact made him squirm, had to walk away. The boy looked forward to summer Saturdays. She had a big mouth, crap attitude, got in trouble a lot, like real trouble. He was envious a little bit. She was overly confident about her good looks, red chili pepper hair, swirling hazel eyes, she never wore a hint of makeup. The years passed, the boy had to look away, fumbling his hands, finding busy work so she didn't catch him blush. See, the boy wasn't brave enough to tell her, ask her out. Until, it would be too late. This is the saddest part of the fable, the stunning, first and lasting love, the girl would never know.

Zack pulled the strapping young man aside and recounted his own version of the fable. His granddaughter was at a crossroad. She had two very different paths to decide, one that would destroy her, the other, the perfect, every wish granted fairy tale life. He knew her life would not be without heartache. He wanted to give her the best shot, hence the garden. He knew about the drugs, hanging out with the worst possible crowd, picking awful guys. She was hurting, lashing out, just like Harry. The thing about girls like her and her grandmother, if they are shown real love they will blossom returning it tenfold. The boy prayed this was the part where he asked him to watch over her, and it was. Only it was very different than what he thought. "I'm dying soon, son. It's time, that's all. Promise me, you'll watch out for her. Check in from time to time. Promise you'll be a true friend. Friend, not a thing more. You'll need a clear head, or she'll barrel you over. Understand, son?" Before he knew, the boy was shaking his head in the absolute, worst, wrong direction. It was a promise he could never keep. He loved her, there was no other path for him.

Georgia was hiding her tears, in shame, regret and wasted years. She idolized her grandfather, loved him more than anyone. She was sobbing now, why hadn't he seen it. Did he? Suspect all along? She didn't understand what he was thinking. She loved Jake.

Jake wiped the tears, and kissed Georgia on the cheek. He understood Zack perfectly.

"Your grandfather was trying to spare us the pain of great, big love. The vacancy Harry left, when she was his world. Not even the love of his favorite, ginger, precocious granddaughter could fix his heart. He thought he could save you the long road, the hurt, he was being Dr. Pretty."

Georgia said nothing. She sat quietly a long while, processing the night, the stars, the man-boy beside her, who had been her one, true friend all along. Even when she was a raging bitch, spat unforgivable things and didn't deserve him. Monitor static, Jax was whimpering. "I'll go," Georgia leaned in. Jake squeezed her hand in the I'm not going anywhere, laid back, capable, Jake fashion, "let me."

Just like that, *insta* family. Not *just* like that, there'd be sinkholes, shit-storms, Santa Ana winds, cussing, door slamming, looming packed duffles. Georgia would retreat to Zack's den and his cardigan, dark solitary nights, weeks, months, curtains drawn, behind locked doors. There would be man-beer in the fridge, tender embraces, adoption papers, school compromises, obligatory grandparent visits, surf lessons, Harry's Digs meetings and more community gardens. Life happenings came that were good, Zack worthy. There would be no exaggerated displays of affection. When Jake took Georgia's hand and squeezed, she knew with the certainty of a steady, Cove summer sunrise he would never let go. Theirs was a great big, worth the wait love.

Birds of Prey

Red-wing blackbirds dropped out of the Louisiana sky onto a highway, thump, thump, thump. Like firecrackers, multiplied. No 'end of the world' alien invasion, disease, poison, there was no logical, scientific explanation. The National Audubon Society confirmed, '*mass bird die-offs are not rare.*' *These large events do take place. It's not terribly unusual.* After midnight, Maxine brushed her teethed, washed her face and changed into the linen nightgown that had been left on the bed that morning. She made a habit of putting morning outfits out the night before and PJs on her bed. She was too tired after a full workday, brain freeze-dried. Tonight, she was unusually exhausted, the store had been filled to capacity with tourists who saw the *O No* write-up, "Ten Hot Stops in The French Quarter."

Poor Mettus, sent him home around ten, on his feet since 5 a.m. He could barely stand, Max worried. Fussed over him, he wasn't a young man. M.T. never told his age, never complained about work. He wasn't young, even middle aged, Maxine guesstimated by the off color stories he told. They dated him, seventies' she bet. Even Eveleen couldn't say, her mama laughed her off. "That man might be 150, all I know."

Maxine rested her heavy head on the down pillow counting back three, two, one…she was out. Her last thoughts before black peace nothingness, thank God she drove past his block, and red-winged blackbirds falling from earth. Shame, she could not rescue them all.

Maxine sprung in her sleep. Clanking. Eagle ears from years of sharing a room with her delinquent sister who snuck out. Georgia would gawk at Max halfway out the sill, and wink. Max never tattled, she stayed awake waiting to hear the familiar thud. Georgia on the carpet, drunk, high, cracking up. "Shoosh," Max grunted leaving her sprawled on the floor to sleep it off and promptly fell back asleep.

She slept with the windows open, loved the gentle, New Orleans cross breeze that floated in from the bayou through the loft. Metal, rattling. Again. Shit, she forgot. Mettus reminded her, three times. She checked the garden, flipped the lights, misted the bamboo, prepped the bar for morning, restocked the books. She forgot, stupid. The chains rattled. Her damn phone, where was it? Frantically emptying her purse, checking the bathroom, kitchen, she left it on the register. She'd done it a thousand times, why now?

Maxine threw on her morning outfit, bra, white linen pants, long sleeve gauze shirt, slipped on Toms and sat on the bed. Maybe they want money, there wasn't much in the drawer. M.T. warned her not to keep too much cash. She heard books being thrown off the shelves, breaking glass, it was frenetic, angry noise. Maxine waited for silence, she'd climb down the fire escape, Eveleen was five doors down. She waited, eyes wide, mouth shut, like she'd waited for Georgia those long nights. Fifteen minutes, silence that's a good sign. Maxine waited an hour, to be sure. She closed her eyes, took a deep breath and tiptoed towards the back window. The image of blackbirds falling from the heavens on her wood floors made the twenty-foot walk impossible to navigate.

Max didn't hear the dark shadow enter the apartment, sneak up behind her. Curious, she thought. She didn't feel his hands around her neck, snapping it, breaking C1 and C2 vertebrae. It is incredibly difficult to kill someone instantly by breaking the neck. As Max began to lose consciousness, her heart slowing, she remembered some nonsensical trivia about "The Lethal Neck Snap" and Hollywood action movies. A man wearing a beanie, filthy ripped t-shirt and jeans dragged Maxine across the floor, hoisting her over his shoulder, head loose like her and her sisters' Raggedy Ann dolls, fighting not to lose consciousness with each jarring step. She pictured her mother's wavy locks, sweet expression, her daddy's smart grin, the twins, her double dolls jumping and skipping along the surf. From her reserved Cove childhood spot, she saw her sister, stubborn, mysterious, radiant Georgia, full grown, crimson locks shooting beams of red afterglow. Standing in the surf with her back to her, gazing faraway, past the ocean. Maxine could not see her anguished face, did not need to. She felt her overwhelming, all consuming, protective loving sister holding her tight, inside the Max safe bubble. She was dying, why she did not know. When the strange man stopped the car by the edge of a body of water, Max was no longer here. Mercifully, she was pixie-dust particles. She watched the bizarre scene unfold from above, fascinated. The man picked up her lifeless body, waded into the swamp and simply released her into the warm, still waters of the bayou. Maxine could not stop watching the backwards baptism ritual of her limp corpse, thin blond hair fanning out over the water, immersed white linen, exposed forearms, hands and bare feet, transparent. She looked like a captivating, exaggerated, haunting, oversize art photo hung on a wall in some *avant-garde* gallery in Chelsea. Maxine would have purchased the surreal piece on site for the loft. Shocked and mesmerized by the disturbing imagery, she understood how the red-wing blackbirds felt. Mutilated without pain, dropping from the sky, only morbidly curious. There was not one drop of blood on her when the currents pulled her out and further under. She understood the off behavior, lonesome childhood, uncomfortable way she had moved through life now as an adult. Death was not hard, heavy, or dark. It was the long sigh release, ease she longed for, had never found.

Maxine sensed a persistent, nagging tug, pulling her away from the drowned body. Harrison Gertrude.

Hello Neighbor

Heaven is not the same for everyone. She guessed it all wrong. Max's heaven consists of white, transparent orbs in varying sizes, forever moving and colliding in the atmosphere. The size is dependent on different things, how good you were on earth, how much you helped or didn't, the lives you touched, sometimes by the crazy difficult, unfair, tragic human you had been. Lucky, unlucky there was an unbalanced, unjust scale. The globes appearing and disappearing without meaning, like jet stream air bubbles bendy, twirling with no obvious direction atop a pool of water. Each night in the exosphere was Max's favorite. White, glowing translucent orbs of unimaginable beauty crowded the sky. She gasped at the miracle called stars. This was her heaven. Each imagination different, every soul created its own. Harry was there, Zack, too. Sometimes their orbs collided, morphed into one. Never too long, there was no longer the need for human connection. Maxine even bumped beanie man once. She saw his catastrophic life, broken mind, spirit, splintered pieces. She would have wept for him if she still had tears. She didn't thankfully, kept drifting along. Oblong, figure of eights, crescent, ellipse, cylinder, spiral, wave, dome shapes danced on her playground. Quirky, playful bumper cars were Max's heaven. She could go poof, dissipate whenever she liked, but she wouldn't. She enjoyed the pretty, serene globes cruising along. Her poor mama, fragmented, shattered, guilt-ridden, worried so, *insanity runs in the family*. What she couldn't know, what she wouldn't know for a brief, fleeting time, was what *felt* like death to her, was actually mortal love living. The orbs are born the same, trying to understand the same emotions, navigate treacherous, wondrous, scary waters, unfamiliar terrain, never pausing for air. Maxine didn't picture her future as a small child, unafraid of what was inevitable. No longer having the option to taste air, she dreamed safety bubbles, glorious white domes instead. Humans presume their orbs are unique, very different, when in fact they are not, they remain very much the same. The only variants are in shape, color and size.

Rue Saint-Denis

Opal bought a one-way ticket to Paris; Air India was the cheapest she found. She wanted to feel the wobbly, uneven cobblestones, experience the yellow light blur Harrison saw. Opal wanted to live in the precise spots she did, spread a blanket in *her* park under the Tour Eiffel with a ham and cheese baguette, sit in her sadness, experience the solitude. Opal wanted to understand her melancholy. Harrison wasn't real, she knew, but the sensory description, people and places were real enough. They made Opal feel brave, adventurous. She kept the guidebook from the library so long she owed three months' late fees. When she slouched to the desk, book in bag, Lucy the librarian, was smiling. She was caramel apple sweet, thrifty mom, a head turner once, who didn't bother with the upkeep. Opal saw the soft, feminine curves hiding under polyester, handsome edges, the pretty features fading. She felt sad. Lucy raised three boys, delinquents on her husband's crap salary, worked all day. She craved a daughter, someone to play dress up, smell pink like cotton candy, a female to do frou-frou and lacy girly things with. Heck, make grocery shopping fun, supper, cleaning the house less tedious. Lucy tried and tried, until the doctor took her insides. Three second-trimester miscarriages scarred her insides for good. She held her dead babes in her arms, tear drops bounced off their blue-gray skin. She finally got her girl, refused to unwrap the tiny corpse swaddled in soft, quiet, crayon color blankie. Lucy caressed her, whispered she'd see her soon, not to be afraid, hummed for a long while. Until the stocky, solemn nurse came, Lucy sobbed, turning to her side, rubbing her vacant belly. She knew, never told. She knew her girl the second their skin touched. Her features were soft, fingers delicate, scrunched button nose. My God she was perfect; Lucy called her Dolly. They didn't have a proper burial, no headstone, Dolly was buried with her brothers in a field behind the house, stiff grass and pebble hill. Lucy never forgave her husband, worthless, lazy, beer-belly drunk. Made him get snipped, threatened to take the boys. Lucy didn't go, she'd already given up.

Her Opal brightened the dusty, dank library walls when she came, which was less and less these days. Lucy replaced the guide months ago, secretly wishing *she* was going somewhere, anyplace there weren't dirty underwear on the hardwood floors, smelly socks to wash, stews to cook, pounds of meat to grill, *anything* non-boyish, unrelated to men. She dreamed of five star hotels in romantic, medieval settings with 600 thread count white linens fresh every day. Her own personal valet, lobster, salmon breakfast quiche, melon, pineapple, and strawberries cut in perfect, round balls. French pressed cafe on real silver, hmmm. Sam Shepard and Sam Elliot, staying in adjacent suites. Not those awful, effeminate movie stars she watched on E! TV. The ones that took *selfies* and stared in camera lens, too busy lovin' on themselves. Never learned how to treat a woman. The drugstore cowboys visited her evenings, read Jane Austen in bed. Shit, she *really* needed to stop her dollar store habit, paperback erotica. It was polluting her brain. Still, it wasn't real, not like she was out screwing twenty-somethings, not like him, dirty bastard husband. Lucy heard the chatterboxes when she stopped at the diner most afternoons, ignored the back-finger pointing.

You do it Opal, travel for me. Get the hell out, go, live fast, love big. She peeked at Seven, day dreaming her per usual quota of vacant looks. That kid.

"Hey, whatcha doin'?"

"I'm sorry Lucy, I..." reaching into her bag, hand extended with the corner turned, page tattered, 80's Flier's guidebook. Opal's cheeks felt guilty. She had twenty-five dollars and eighty-nine cents, tapping her boot against the checkout desk, fraught with nervous energy.

"Hey, quit kicking the desk, scuff marks. I *just* polished it. That old thing," indicating the guide- book. "Keep it, it's a decade outdated, ordered a current edition awhile back."

"Sure?" Opal adjusts her rims, lets out a long sigh fixating on a bleeding ink spot in the wood separating them, shuffling her feet. When she was little, her dad would drop her here after school.

On quiet days, which came often in rural villages, summertime library allure can't compete with a Kindle. Shame on evolution, Lucy loved cracking a spine, crisp crackling paper, tactile feel, the weight of holding a book. She kept an antique typewriter on her bedroom desk, liked the clickety clack, dinging bell and how her fingers had to push down harder on the keys, making her think. Lucy imagined the literary genius,' typing the classics on an Underwood, Halda or Remington. Hemingway, Faulkner, Plath hunched over computers.

"Silly," she grunted. Utter nonsense. Cormac McCarthy typed his novels on a Lettura 32 Olivetti, won a Pulitzer Prize. Sold at auction for $250,000, almost *ten* times her house. Lucy was a romantic, a reader who wished she could write. She was old-fashioned, traditional and that was her way. She plopped down on the carpet alongside a young Seven, reading Judy Blume.

Opal craved the close proximity, how her hair smelled of talc, the starchy, stiffness of her paisley shirt, how giddy she got when it brushed her bare arm. On days when it was disgusting, ick hot, the town kids whooped and hollered, running under sprinklers. Opal preferred the musty smell of oak, 360-degree view of spines, neatly filed shelves, and the familiar gray comfort of curly cue, carpet thread. When it was the two of them, engrossed in *Alice in Wonderland,* she liked that best. Opal liked to pretend Lucy was her mom.

11:11

Georgia starts from the annoying, telephone ring in a cozy, cocoon dream state, tries to ignore it. FUCK! Telemarketers, they'd wake Jax. She fumbled in the dark of their bedroom, reaching over Jake's nude, tight torso searching for the phone. Picking it up, slamming it down, she counted. One, two, three, not a peep. Jax was teething, poor miserable boy. Georgia tried frozen peas, paci, organic popsicles, baby Motrin, nada. The last week Georgia slept in the nursery, rocking, singing, trying to calm him. Nodding off in the rocker, her bubbly boy gone, left with a grumpy, miserable baby cradled in her arms. She caved, rubbed Whiskey on his gums, to hell with organic. Ten minutes, he was out.

"Yes," she blurted covering her mouth, placing him in his crib. She didn't believe the twins whiny complaints as new moms. In bed by 8:30, horseshit. Maybe, she'd get three hours if she snuck down the hall, climbed under the duvet. Jake tried, watched Jax a few nights, sucker. Came home from work like a shriveled turnip, speaking gibberish. She'd switch places, go to Harry's Digs, but she liked days at the beach with Jax way too much. He was quite the little surfer, thank God he loved the water as much as she.

Five, ten, twenty shrills, damn ringer.

"Christ, pick up," shaking Jake's torso, kicking him awake. "Hello."

Georgia sat up, switched the light to see him, voice sounded weird. He'd been silent on the phone too long, "hmm, um, mhmhhh." What the fuck was *that*, something wasn't right, his forehead creased, eyes cloudy. She felt fear drip off his sweaty chest. The baby monitor blinked red, Georgia ignored the warning, clutching Jake's trembling forearm. The peculiar way he looked at her, Georgia had never seen before. She snatched the phone out of his hand, and listened. Adelaide, it was her mother's breathing. Something was very, very bad. Georgia spent a lifetime living with her mother, knew all her sounds. The unwelcome *unfirst*, Adelaide couldn't speak, rumbling, pausing, followed by a laborious, low rumble. It was the most terrifying sound she ever heard. The sound a mamma elephant makes standing over her dead baby. Primordial, the jungle's sacred burial ground at low frequency.

"MOTHER," Georgia screamed hoping to jar her back. "Where's daddy?" heartbeat quickening. You're scaring the shit out of me." Jax was wailing down the hall, Georgia ignored it, the telephone her only lifeline. Jake threw on a t-shirt, bottoms and pointed at the door. She nodded, grateful. Georgia should tell him she loved him, buy him something. Stupid, who was she kidding?! Jake didn't need a soapbox derby. This was him and her.

"Mommy, don't hang up," rolling her eyes. She couldn't remember the last time she called her Mommy. Sounded funny and disturbing. Georgia checked the clock, 11:11 pm. Good juju. Maxine was forever *over-sharing* her spiritual insights. Wacky, spooked, metaphysical random shit only *she* would know. Secretly, Georgia kinda' liked it. She wanted desperately to believe in Max' fascinations, her ghosts, spirits, numerology, reflexology, astrology, tarot cards, meditation, juice fasts. The gazillion spiritual quests her sister explored were exhausting.

Georgia was practical, like their mother. Charting life by the ebb and flow of the tides, sunrise, sunset and the earth's rotation.

She trusted the currents, undertow, roiling waves and the sea's ever-changing moods. She depended on the next break, the timing, how much algae, white froth and shells washed ashore. The Cove was her identity, the place she longed for when absent, the home she belonged to. It was her tapestry, ancestry, spirit, soul and mind. Calcite, turquoise, cobalt, red- tides, and blue omnipresence evening glow, her legacy. She could never exist land-locked, her breath would wilt from sorrow without a body of water in close proximity. Georgia stood, looked out the window at infinity below, trying to spot a speck of light to ground her, grasping tight to the receiver. She watched the waves, listening to each break, counting on the next. Poor Jake. Jax was howling, hang up. Go. Georgia couldn't break the connection, leave her mother terrified, sitting in the dark somewhere in her childhood home. Georgia was losing control twisting a strand of hair, hard. She had two minutes she guessed, before she screamed. One and half, pulling hard. Sixty…thirty pulling harder…fifteen…five...broken crimson lock in hand…

"Max," Adelaide's voice hoarse from exhaustion and tears.

Georgia released the vice grip on her hair, blowing the strand into the air. This is good. It's Max.

"I just talked to her yesterday, I think?" Shit, day before, counting back the days on her fingers. Frustrated, they strung together, fuzzy. Sleep deprived, Jax' screams. She needed Shiva or Octopus hands. "We Skyped. The garden, Jax was making a holy, dirty mess with a shovel. I'm sure. Max was cracking up." Georgia shook her head, typical Maxine flake-out bullshit.

"There was a break-in, Mettus called 911. Good Scents vandalized, shelves knocked down, broken glass, books ripped apart, the garden, it's gone. Adelaide was whimpering. "The loft wasn't touched, not a thing. She hasn't been home, three days. You know her, how she detests change." Full on ugly sobs, gasping for air.

"Three days, Georgia. I'm going to the airport at dawn, catching the first flight, straight to the police station. Oh, Daddy's fine, sweetheart. I'm sorry I scared you. He's staying, in case she calls."

"It's Max, mom. *Jesus Christ*, I told her to chill with the goodwill, save the world crap. I'm packing." Georgia frantically flings open the closet doors, throws a duffle on the bed, opens the dresser and tosses in mismatched sweaters, tees, undies, jeans and a still unpacked toiletry kit from the last visit.

"Call Mettus, he'll come to the airport. Meet at the store, wait for me. I want to check the loft, see if something is missing before the cops." The phone dead, her mother is gone.

Georgia tiptoed to the bathroom to wash her face, brush her teeth. She caught her reflection in the mirror, falling in slow motion, reaching behind her. Searching for something, anything to brace the fall. Sprawled on the slate tile, dry heaving, hugging the toilet bowl was cool and calming. She wished she would throw up, acid retching, burning her throat. This was not some sixteen-year-old, black orchid tattoo delinquent prank, teen angst army pant, tough girl, smart mouth, know it all plea; this was not testing their mother's limits. Not the five-year-old naked body smeared in paint, good girl Max sticking out her tongue taunting. Was Georgia sick, out of her mind? *This* was Max and this was not like Max at all. Jake held Georgia's hair with one arm, Jax curled in the other.

"Babe, I gotta go," letting go of the vice grip, ceramic support. Jake wanted to lift her, carry her to their bed, solid ground. Afraid she might slug him, he remained calm. Jake saw the twirls of yellow terror in Georgia's eyes, head in the toilet. She was a warrior, amazed by how capable she was. Except, when it came to family. Her family. Georgia became softer, prettier, hair shinier, belly laughed out-loud. He and Jax were lucky to experience all the bountiful *facets* that were Georgia. Swimmer's physique, soft mother's arc, lioness, protector, independent, organic, natural, unpredictably sweet, malleable edges. Jake never tired of the rotating, varied depths of Georgia.

"Go, we'll be fine." Jake held out his hand. Georgia twisted her hair in a bun, reaching to meet him. Day was near, she could feel the warm sunlight, climbing over the bluff to greet them. Up all night. She'll kill her if Max is on yet another enlightening retreat, no cellphones, forgot to mention. She prayed. Georgia half smiled at Jake, stroked Jax's soft forehead. She nodded, letting Jake know that was his cue to beat it, she was late. She brushed her teeth, again, dialed the cab service, ordered a car and kept moving. Fifteen minutes, shit. Triple checked her purse; all she really needed were credit cards, cash and driver's license.

White Linen and Pretty Things

"Her pajamas aren't on the bed, clothes for the morning." Her mother's quiet, terrifying observation bounced off the brick walls. That initial, simple sentence followed them for years, like an abused, tick-filled, mange-ridden, abandoned, starved puppy.

When they pulled in front of Good Scents, hundreds of people lined the street, white candles, white flowers and white ribbons adorned the street. Georgia buried her emotions under her tresses. The plastic table set with pots of gumbo and Dixie cups. The locals she fed were serving others, pouring soup. The love pulsating off that sidewalk was white kindness, pure Max. *"YOU would have adored it,"* Georgia spoke to the air, the celeste sky, the unattractive, brown waters hoping the words would find her.

They ask too much, expect more from me. To sit with gut wrenching, broken, beaten down souls. There is too much pain upon the blood, stained walls. I cannot, I will not. I refuse to spill my intimate, tragic, sad story. This fight is personal, entirely my own. Between God and me, my sister is not the enemy. I wonder, I do. I can't help but be curious, where did the cracks start? The precise second the earth blew, were the leaks there all along?

Sweat trickling down her neck, Georgia's fire tresses caught the orange sun's late afternoon glow, somber and stunning. Once a year, she returns. Stands firm, Wellington's planted where mud meets water. Louisiana swampland, mossy bayou, a green so vibrant she cannot describe the magnificent beauty. Massive cypress' musk air, painstakingly slow, gator-filled muddy waters. Easter bunny blue sky and cotton, puff clouds her reflecting pools. It's been two decades, since Max. Twenty years, missing every peculiar, odd, quirk about her. The pain dull, anger reconciled, guilt the unhealthy hanger on, sick reminder. What if she stayed, didn't go back to the Cove? The pitiful image of Max blubbering, clinging to the cab window made her cold from the inside. Prying her fingers off the glass, she couldn't know. The last touch, the hideous, finite, can't go back and fix, physical memory. Georgia spent years flying between the Cove and the Bayou. She hung flyers, drove in circles, drank bourbon neat, tracked miles and miles, asking, insisting, searching the Quarters, bayous, pounding doors. She, the warrior, could not accept no answers, to lose Max over and over. The first day Adelaide brought her sweet, quiet, bald baby home, Georgia stood guard over her crib for hours. That was the way it was, their way, Max and her. Georgia's identity without Maxine didn't fit.

When Mettus died, a very, very, very old man, Eveleen phoned crying. Moments before he left, tears stained corners of weathered eyes, followed by a great big, holy-moly, happy grin. Grouchy, stern Mettus never smiled. Eveleen swore *she* was in that room, Mettus only smiled for Max. Georgia left M.T. the store; he arrived every morning before dawn, laid out sandwiches. It was good, what Max would have wanted.

Eveleen was a grown woman, with babies and a solid, hard working husband. She stayed on at the store expanding the menu and bar, removing the books. Nobody read real books, shaking her head. She made a fine living, far from the hungry $5.00 days, busing tables. Eveleen kept Max' books in storage, left the décor and magic gardens as they were, bamboo twenty feet tall, for when Max returned. Georgia gifted her the deed years ago. Eveleen cried and cried, willing Maxine to walk through the door, luminescent in flowing white and an over-size fringe shawl, only slightly aged from the arduous journey, more radiant than before. Eveleen still phoned before making any changes.

It's funny Max, maybe we never get to know the lives we touched until we're gone. You my new age, ghost whisperer, forgiver, fixer, independent, sister of my soul, touched too many. You were never afraid to be. I hated that, mostly because I was jealous. Twenty years, Max. I get it, I love all your puzzle parts, even the ones that made me bat shit crazy.

Trade Winds

Georgia knows her sister is gone. But this act, coming to the bayou, talking to Maxine has become her sacred ritual. She pulls her cardigan over her bare shoulder, covering the faded ink, black orchid tattoo. The air is warm and wet, trade winds breeze through bringing her sister with them. She talks to her at the Cove, about stuff, whatever, daily nonsense, pulling weeds, Jake, Jax, Zelda and Trudy, aging parents. Georgia hopes she listens; some days are black and she can't find any trace of Max. That first year she had a new baby and lover. She wanted to be happy; her heart was dead. Georgia was resilient, she understood better with time and distance. Dedicated her days to her son, Miss Barbara's legacy, cheerios, almond milk, fresh smoothies, hearty green vegetables, beach play dates, long boards, salt, sea naps, vitamin D rays, tubbies, picture books, footie hulk pajamas, rocker, lullaby, bottle, nighty, night. She did all the things a good mother does, without joy. The block Lego astronaut missing the guts and emotion.

Jake. She couldn't hide from him, too many years. He recognized each of her walks, expressions, what it meant when she rolled her neck to the left or to the right. He said nothing, loved harder in Jake's easy, calming way. Georgia walked into the kitchen, reaching for a tumbler and Maker's Mark. He didn't shift in the chair, grazing her back with his hand as she passed. Georgia retreated to Zack's den, slipped on his brown cardigan with the ragged elbow patches. Sinking inside the faded, cracked leather sofa, sipping brown liquid, drowning 300 feet above the ocean. One glass Max, only one. 365 days, four seasons blurred into gray nothingness. Until Jake stood, menacing hand out, between her and the bottle. "Enough."

Georgia collapsed howling, Jake wrapped his entire able body, legs, feet, arms and hands around her. Georgia felt the trade winds blow warm from the screen porch. Okay Max, *okay*. She had to let Jake in, help manage the grief, guilt and fear if they were to survive.

Tangy Tart BBQ

Summer breaks, Gertrude, Z-Z and their children migrated to the Cove. They didn't call, there was no formal invitation. They returned with their parents to the mystic, healing beach. Revisiting the past, naïve, carefree childhood days where they were most happy. Zack was there, Harrison too in memory. Together, they were whole and however briefly, it sustained them. Sisters were lucky, beach babies, silly girls, unpredictable adolescents, allowed to grow, thrive, fight, hate, and love, forever bound by family. Max kicked and screamed come summer's end, not wanting to say good-bye. She was most content, most comfortable, most alive on that beach. So they came, the physical need to be together trumped the miles apart, schedule conflicts, prior commitments. Jax ran around for weeks, "the cousins, the cousins!" Jake and Caden pitched tents off the porch, the boys snuck worms from the compost, tucked under the girls' pillows. The adults didn't mind, the shrieks, roars and laughter were welcome reminders of the carefree sounds of youth.

Jake or Caden grilled hotdogs, hamburgers, Zack's 'catch of the day,' the twins washed leafy lettuce, vegetables Jake brought from Harry's Digs. Georgia's gardens decomposed, left untouched. Georgia refused to tend to them until Max came home. The kids tossed half-eaten, paper plates in the bin, belly's full, tuckered from the sun, waves and heat. Lighting lanterns, they whispered tales of ghosts and sea monsters. The grownups sat at the picnic table, drinking too much, crying, laughing, swearing, cursing, reliving 'Max' stories. "Remember when, she...kicking and screaming..." As if somehow the sharing might bring her back. Adelaide listened, glazed, vacant. She wasn't there with her family.

Addie was envisioning herself by the water, searching for her mother, in Harry's rocker, on her bed, Harrison holding her daughter's anguish in her hands. She needed her mother to tell her what to do, where to put all the pain. Addie wanted Harrison. It was simple; mother's fix things, stomachaches, deepest cuts, terrifying nightmares. She was lost. She needed Harry to lie, tell her child was alive; she knew it wasn't true. A mother knows, a mother knows first. Maybe Harry was with Max, that's why she didn't come. Poor Georgia, Adelaide looked at her defeated daughter, worry lines deeper overnight. She won't stop, poor baby. Fists cupped under her chin, the sea goddess, gypsy blond mane, loose and wild, reached cautiously for Georgia's hand across the table. "*YOU* are not responsible my crimson child, this is not your burden." Georgia's face contorted, sucking back tears, freeing her hand, bolting towards the beach. She hated her for giving up, weak, useless. Georgia lifted the heaviest, black, jagged diamond rock she could find in the dark, hurling it far into the ocean burning her biceps and slicing open palms.

"FUCKING BITCH. I'LL NEVER QUIT, MAX," crazed, scorching cheeks ten shades deeper than her out of control hair. Adelaide rose, walked to the edge of the bluff where heaven meets water watching her firstborn hurl boulders at the sea. She, Georgia Pine's mother, could not *fix* this, as much as the hypocrite prayed, bartered. She believed in the ancient seas, gale winds moving massive bodies of water, gyrating currents, riptides, undertows and fell to her knees clasping her hands.

Increments

Georgia sits in the rocker on the porch, arms crossed tight. The red wave locks, fury spilling over her shoulders, matches the fire building inside. There was life with Max, and everything after. Too many years between Maxine and now, Georgia could not accept. She did not ask to be guardian, warrior, the protector, Maxine's guide. The kindred sister spirit role decided long ago on the stars Max so adored. Georgia did not breathe easy after Max, they shared the same air. Spiritual yin and yang, she was her right lung. The days, endless, dutiful without Max. She was a good mother, kissed Jax' wounds, cleaned and bandaged them. Provided the green nutrients he would need for a healthy life. She could not dare give him her whole heart, terrified. Georgia made love to Jake in their bed, watching the stars out the window scanning the night, for her. Oxygen, signs from her baby sister. The guilt of leaving Maxine behind, consumed her. Bottled up rage, ripping and scratching, left her insides bloodied and raw. Georgia never lived fully the joy, existing instead. Tuesdays, Wednesdays, and Thursdays came on repeat. Maxine was never of this world, but in it. She was the transient light that shines so lovely, you cannot help but be swept up by the ethereal beauty. She was *her* person, and Georgia refused to count the minutes, life after Max. Days didn't matter, sunrises came and sunsets went, earth kept right on rotating. Georgia measured life in increments, with Max and without. She looked at the crisp, clear, impossible silver sky, wiped the one tear allowed and knew. She understood in her cells, matching DNA, the fire burning in her gut, Maxine was out there. The incandescent light, dancing and smiling hello. Georgia knew exactly what her sister would whisper, "I wish you could see this place, it's glorious. Magic. The increments go fast, Georgia Pine. Let it go. Crimson is the brightest, most devoted hue. I know you know." Georgia puts away the guilt, sorrow, rage and wallowing for the night. Most days, her amazing, blessed family fills the gap.

Silver Spoon Baking

Summer tradition remained. Adelaide and Caden, Z-Z and Trudy, significant others and available kids came. Jax was a sweet boy, kind, athletic, playful and thoughtful much like Zack, most like Jake. He had fragments of Georgia, Tabasco personality, willful and confident. The *teen-angster*, no longer leaped when his cousins visited *(duh, uncool Ma)*, rolled his eyes while pitching tents. The farther time got away, the shorter Max tales became, less enthusiastic. Her name mentioned, *on occasion*. Maybe hopelessness wore them down, each developing their own coping mechanisms, personal grieving. She was present in every room, cookout, crumbling step, each rare, sand quartz crystal. She became 'the thing' that went missing, the heirloom baking spoon you can't find ransacking the kitchen. The crooked, carved name, 'Maxine' etched in the picnic table, corroded from salt air and ruthless sunshine, mindlessly retraced by curious fingers. No one stopped loving, missing, wanting the precious, cherished, desirable thing they can't live without. They live less vibrantly, less happy, less full, less Max. Her people never quit rummaging through kitchen cabinets, turning over loose rocks, looking for a sign. Absentminded, retracing her name in the unvarnished, antiquated picnic table over morning coffee. The passage of time and distance make the missing less blinding. So life can go on until the vanished, tarnished, treasured spoon mysteriously reappears, hiding out in the back of a drawer. Like it had always been there, making you wonder.

Georgia looked forward to one week with *her* family, missing them more when they were in her presence. She knew they would go, leaving behind Cove memories, and a vacancy in her heart.

Sia

Once a year over the past twenty years, Georgia returns. To New Orleans, the city of drawl darlings, Spanish moss, po-boys, old charm, voodoo magic, trumpeters and garish metallic. The world Maxine visited in her childhood dreams, the one place she felt at home. Georgia stood in the mossy bayou swamp, the exact spot Maxine stood before, water lapping against her boots. The visits became habitual, the melancholy necessity, something she had to do. Today, she no longer made the trek alone.

See, Max I'm not so stoic, proud, stubborn speaking to her sister through the thin veil of black, gray clouds obscuring a low, mauve, orange setting sun. She pulled her sweater tight around her neck, shifting her stance. Feeling a persistent tug on her pantleg, like a juvenile Red fish fighting hard to break free, hook in mouth. The sweetest, pearly voice with a teeny twang sung, "Mama, it's cold."

Boots sunk in mush, lost in bayou blues, Georgia forgot. Gazing down at the wispy blonde, fair-haired, spike crop, twenty-seven freckles between her nose and across plump cheeks, cherry stain lips grinning up, hands on her hips, tiny fingers tapping Georgia's calf. How could she forget, the darling being Max sent UPS?

"Two minutes, Sia," Georgia removed her bulky, cashmere cardigan and wrapped it snug around the adorable, sweetest little human she'd ever seen.

Sia. Part sea, part LouiSIAna. She was the impossible, her and Jake tried, nothing. Georgia blamed her grief, guilt, rotten ovaries. It was fine; she had her guys. Jax was fifteen, she was middle-aged and Jake was talking retirement. Harry's Digs ran without him, he wanted to travel like they planned. Before the steamroller baby, and well, you know the rest Max.

Jax was a busy kid, skateboarding at the pipes with his dudes, staying at a friend's. Georgia was relieved he wasn't a delinquent like her, no drugs, alcohol, a straight edge.

A blanket, happy half-moon, desolate beach, bottle of tequila, brie, parmesan, salami, figs… and the focaccia you loved, Max. I was um, little drunk, Jake a little too hot. Imagine, ewe, don't! Lying on the blanket, nude, slippery, I looked up. Not out, at the night. A white flash shot across the sky, gone before I shook him. Buried my face inside the crook of Jake's extended arm, wondering where the hell he came from. I forgot Max, got busy with life, you know. Jax wanted to learn to drive. Uncovered pop's truck, holy shit, it feels different from the other side. No wonder mom and dad asked Zack. Heart a friggin' tack. You didn't forget.

Max, she has Harry's spunk, mom's love of the sea and easy, intuitive way with people. Sia makes everyone feel comfortable, her joy contagious. She's stubborn when she needs, and overly confident like her mama. She can be quieting sometimes, introspective, like Jake. Jax? Oh, he adores his baby sister, hands off.

You know all of her smartass; I conceived that night. I still can't believe something that wondrous, that precious, that perfect could happen to Jake and I. Jake beams when he holds her, melts when Sia is near.

When she was born, and opened her big, blue icicle eyes they looked right through me. They're your eyes, Max. When Sia bounds down the hall and jumps in our bed, they smile and shine. When she's sad, angry, hurt, tears spill, way too young to understand. Sia's soulful, knowing eyes tell me different. She belongs to the earth and beyond, the secret mystery. Sia is partially mine, the other, all you. I never thought I was capable of big, big, consuming, white light love until, you. Until, I lost you.

And, found her. My sea baby, LouiSIAna southern girl, the sun bursts through her heart. Sia makes missing you less heavy. She's pirate gold, conquistador treasure, homespun, the finest of the Cove women. Max, life was overcast in sunny Cali' without you. Thank you for coloring my sky with Sia, a pretty 70 degree not a cloud blue, every day of the year.

Georgia's face drenched with tears, ginger locks humid and frizzy from the swamp air. She bends down to lift her overtired, restless, hungry girl holding her close, cheek to cheek.

"Room service, baby?" Georgia doesn't hesitate; turn back to the reflecting pools of Max. She pulls Sia tighter, promising they'll be back.

Sia wiggles, giggles and fidgets excitedly in Georgia's arms, "SHRIMPIE'S and SHIRLEY TEMPLES!!!"

Bodies of Water

Zelda arrived first, before Adelaide. Georgia waved, standing outside the pickup. Airport terminals, baggage claim, exit signs her least favorite destination, she hated the comings and goings. Jax was leaving in twenty-one days, medical school in New York, halfway across the country. Pops must be beaming that Dr. Pretty high voltage grin. Georgia opened her arms, greeting her baby sister. "How's mom?"

"She's, I don't know… mom?" Zelda had sprinted the ten blocks from her house to their mother's, as soon as she called. Adelaide was freakishly quiet, the calmest she'd ever seen her. Her first boyfriend, lover, partner, ocean explorer, grief counselor, husband and father of her babies dead, upright in his recliner, reading a magazine on Biodiversity. No, no, no that's wrong.

Zelda missed the porch steps, flung the door open, ran smack into the gurney and EMTS taking him. "STOP!" screaming hysterical, blocking the door. Zelda lifted the sheet, he felt stiff, skin gray, not blue, like in the movies. They lied.

"Daddy," Z-Z shook him, rested her head on his chest, kissing his lukewarm forehead. Adelaide watched from the hall, curious and confused, solid teak doorframe holding her up. The spectator, she could not go to her daughter, nothing left to give death. Caden exercised, ate green, didn't smoke, drank two beers a month, Jesus fucking Christ. Dropped dead reading a stupid, boring, goddamn science magazine. Zelda was on the floor in fetal position, howling. Adelaide cemented to the wall, too goddamn pissed. Caden never cried in front of his girls, carried his grief inside the rawhide, weathered briefcase. Young Adelaide, his ethereal, adventurous gypsy, carried creases and crevices marking the years together, badges of sorrow.

"I tried, Georgia. She sent me ahead, needed her alone time. So stubborn." Zelda fluttered her lip, releasing a sigh.

"Mom was eighteen when they met, got preggers, married, had me, Max, then you and Trudy too, Harry died, and pops. Losing Max crushed her. She's never been *alone*. It's a lot." As fast as she said the words, Georgia couldn't believe they came out. They fought, *well* Georgia fought. After New Orleans, the first trip to Good Scents, the loft, police station, Adelaide had zero fight. She listened.

"We are tied to the ocean. And when we go back to the sea, whether it is to sail or to watch - we are going back from whence we came." John F. Kennedy.

Adelaide lived by that quote. She refused a god that created anguish, imbalance, hunger, chaos, evil, cancer. The ocean's quietude, eco balance, weightless serenity she trusted, each time her body dove below the surface. She understood the harmonious beauty and magic of a world she could not inhabit, only visit. Harrison blew in her newborn's face, submersing her under the bouncy, refreshing, salt water introducing Adelaide to a secret love they would share. She wished she had gills so she could stay longer, twisting and twirling making bubbles. She was at home with marine life, coral crystalline, and sun's shadow play, funny shapes, and perfect design. The sea goddess would say good-bye, *for now*. She would exist without him on land, but not in the vast, mysterious, expanse of water that filled her heart. Caden was her true friend, partner, deep-water diver, present sea buddy. He gave her four lovely, unique, exquisite creatures. Caden was a tender husband, constant father and gentleman who found a good wave in every ride.

Georgia wanted to paddle out, family. Like always. Gertrude wasn't coming. Her daughter was thirty-eight weeks, she was going to be abuela. *A grandmother.* The twins were little girls speaking a made-up language two minutes ago, Georgia reminisced. Trudy wanted her Z-Z, they cried into computer screens, sorry she couldn't be in two places with one heart. Zelda understood, forever tangled to her twin, living apart. Gertrude loved being a domestica, wife, mom, Spanish markets, empanadas, white asparagus, jamon, gazpacho, flan, sangria, sofrito, paprika, paella, even roast chicken tasted better in Europe. Zelda promised to visit, knowing she wouldn't. Addie smiled, proud of the capable strong mothers, wives and daughters they'd become. Caden, *you* bathed them, read to them, held them, tickled them when I had nothing, overwhelmed and plain worn out. Look at the miracles that are your exquisite daughters, look at what you've done.

Addie went to her divine, brooding ginger daughter, placing her chin in her hand, moving it back and forth, a playful but firm no.

"Not this time."

Nutella and Nectarines

The house was quiet, Jake took Sia to the nursery. Jax was working extra shifts, college cash- stash. He hid a bunch of sunflowers behind a shrub, Sia went charging down the aisle playing along. "I bet they're…," sunny, petite voice disappearing behind the geraniums. Jake nudged Jax, he was going to miss having this guy around. He was going to miss his son.

Georgia and Zelda prepared a picnic basket with their dad's favorites, peanut butter, Nutella, nectarines, grilled jumbo shrimp, Italian bread, a twelve-pack of Red Stripe. Chuckling, while filling the basket, they knew it would taste horrible. Dad liked crazy, weird combinations. Z-Z brought her Smartphone, Trudy wanted to be with there, with them. She didn't care if it was the middle of the night. Drunk, moaning on the blanket with stomachaches, they called their sister. Adelaide gave Georgia the urn and her blessing to each scatter a handful. "Sun's going," Georgia sat up hugging her knees wishing she had Gas X, "alright?" Zelda shook her head, sat on her knees, lips quivering and eyes melting. "Alright." Georgia reached over her sister for the urn, cautiously lifting it with both hands, unscrewing the lid. She reached in eyes closed, grabbing a handful of bone fragments. Georgia read the pamphlet Addie left by the bed, ashes weren't 'dust' at all, they were fragments of bone weighing between three and nine pounds. Creepy she thought, we leave the same weight we are born. Georgia opened Zelda's hand, pouring half into her shaking palm, "*okay?*" Zelda's tears were falling into her palm, she wasn't Georgia, she didn't get that the wet bits of fragments in her hand were her daddy. Georgia reached inside the plaid, flannel button down, front pocket for the phone with her left hand, balancing with the right she stood up waiting on Zelda. Walking the twenty feet from blanket to the sea gave Georgia more minutes, moments shared. Him, sitting on the porch steps in Maine, tired from the long day, never too tired to sit and watch his girls run around the yard, squealing, rolling in the grass. Caden's golden surf locks, kind eyes, strong arms carried his babes up the stairs at bedtime, baths. When he sat sullen, hunched on a bench, waiting for the one jail cell to open, broken daughter inside, he did not flinch, yell. He met her scared eyes with patient, loving, "everything's going to be fine" ones. Caden never raised his voice, adored his girls, omnipresent, rooting and cheering with no judgment. When she handed Jax to him, her daddy cried, holding his grandson tight. He greeted Jake with a firm handshake, and a wink in her direction. Max, when Max went missing, he swallowed his pain to care for a grieving wife and wrecked children. "Oh daddy, you were never invisible, we were too loud. I couldn't find her; I tried. Your gigantic, beautiful heart carried us all. Tell her, oh, *you know*..."

Georgia and Zelda looked at each other through foggy eyes, releasing their palms. Caden's fragments sat on top of the water; he needed time. To process, breathe in his stunning creatures, half moon sky and twenty-point sun. Caden was a thoughtful, simple man surrounded by a female vortex of movement. He was almost home, the current pulling him under the aquatic world. His favorite place *well,* second. West coast mountains, torrential downpours stuck in a tent for days with *her*, the young girl, on a dive with his gypsy goddess, parading the newborn twins around town, Z-Z strapped to his back and Trudy on his chest. Watching Georgia teach Jax to swim, snuggle time with Maxine, inhaling her damp, delicious hair, fresh from a bath. Caden's love for *that life*, trumped all. Georgia flipped the screen so they could see her; blubbering Gertrude was blowing her nose with a hanky holding a flashlight. Z-Z burst out laughing. Georgia punched her in the arm, hard, cracking up. All three of them laughing so hard they were crying, Georgia and Zelda dropped to the sand, Georgia's arm extended holding the phone above the waves. "Hey, watch it, stupid," Zelda shouted, between giggles. As the last fragment of their father disappeared below the surface, Caden was thrilled to see his girls happy again. They were going to be fine, they had each other. He saw a glow from the back bedroom window in the house, lingering wavy tresses, the familiar silhouette watching. He knew Adelaide was smiling.

Wet on a Glass

X stared at the water beads forming outside the glass, drip, drip, drip. The paper towel perspiring leaving a wide, wet berth. Her throat swelled, tongue dry, sure she was choking on fear and uncertainty. The numbness in her limbs, face, extremities, droopy eye, beads of sweat forming across her forehead were her constant panic companions. Her body paralyzed, X's mind spins out of control. She was in full tilt-a-whirl mode, mind and body screaming to break free. Unable to get out of bed, X was frozen with fever, chills, muscle aches, engorged neck, phantom toes on fire, forearms, wrists, temples, jaw clenched pulsating with pain. She longed for death, the pill bottle taunting her mere inches from the bed. X willed her hand to move, the chore of living could be over. She was a coward hiding behind make-believe, rich, complex, worthy lives. Descriptive heroines who were nothing like the pathetic gimp, insignificant being she was. X could not stop the wet on the glass or her tears, wasn't sick or dying. She was past sad, engulfed in the deep, drowning in angry black seas powerless to use her arms and swim to the top. The light had always been there, but not for her. X believed she was not worthy, there was no grand future. She was the nuisance, worse than the pile of shit that reeked and festered, soiling her sheets. X was the deformed despicable maggot, greedy vile bottom feeder crawling under her skin.

Doubly devastated, mourning the loss of her mother, coping mechanisms, and her imaginary friends. Harrison's vibrant, envious, glorious world had been hers on loan, the chapters closing. X can't keep Harry, she was never hers to begin with. Harrison was the bold, brash, perfect, imperfect, made-up character creation she wished she was. The who she imagined out of the chair, away from the self-confined espresso walls and paralyzing, exhausting, inexplicable fear. X reached for her squashed matted down baby pillow, flattened a dull white from too many wash cycles. Vice gripping the sheets, it did little good to quash the swells of anxiety. The night and shallow breathing were not her friends. The palpable unbearable pain and loneliness were her sick twisted lovers and loyal bed companions. Her grief, regret, remorse, shame, self-hatred and ugly sorrow were the dampness she could not shake or wipe away. X despised every single sorry inch of herself. Breaking free from the negative prison patterns of her twisted double-bolted mind, seemed insurmountable.

X freed Harrison from the confines of her shattered mind, the self-imposed paralysis. The chair wasn't her problem, they made prosthetics that could run, jump and yes, walk. The problem was X. There was no way to spin it, she had to leave the Cove and the insulated fantasy. Wet beads on a glass can be wiped down, non-fevers broken, and spirits lifted. *It is what it is.* She hated when her mother said that, and she said it a lot.

Blue is the Loveliest Color

Caden was a Marine Biologist. He knew the statistics, babies are born 75% water, brains are three-fourths water. The ancients came out of the water swimming, crawling, then walking. Early development fetuses have 'gill-slits' structures and the brain rests in a clear, colorless fluid. His brilliant, scientific mind understood blue was the loveliest color. He was going home ahead of her and that blue felt maudlin.

The water in our cells is "comparable to the sea." When you see the ocean, you know you're in the right place. Adelaide put on her wetsuit, checked her personal scuba gear, the guide had a tank. Caden had torn a page from a surf magazine, tacking it to the kitchen bulletin board twenty years ago. "25 Best Places To Go Scuba Diving." They only made two, Blue Hole in Belize and Kailua Kona, Hawaii. Stingrays, giant sea turtles, whales and tropical fish in colors so vibrant, she wept. There'd be time he smirked, with Georgia and Max in diapers. Addie grimaced when the ultrasound technician flipped the monitor in their direction beaming, "twins!" Christ, they'd never leave the house again. The page tattered, worn, 'hot spots' outdated, she gently pulled the tack, folding her husband's bucket list, placing it inside her wallet. For tomorrow would be their last sea adventure.

Georgia was waiting in the truck to drive her mom to the dock. Dingy booked complete with guide, noon to five. Why the hell did she need five hours? Adelaide carried her basic gear to the porch, wetsuit tied around her slender waist. She looked like a young girl, a local, sea salt knotting her golden, untamed locks. Georgia had forgotten the Cove was *her* world, the one she shared willingly with her daughters. The blue mystery they returned to, the ruler not for measuring height or weight, only growth. To learn, eat, play, swim, lounge, surf, nurture and to love by the sea.

"Sure?" Georgia observed her mom unloading the gear. Dingy man nodded 'a what's up old friend.' Georgia felt a sting of envy.

"Georgia, this young fellow captained the yacht at our wedding. You were there." Adelaide rubbed her belly, recognizing her daughter's pouty expression. "Get, go. Back at 5:oo?"

Georgia nodded. Sulking like Sia when she doesn't get her way.

Adelaide held the rope, pointing to the horizon. Wade started the engine, no direction necessary. He would steer to the farthest, deepest, safest spot. Like when they were kids.

Addie raised her fist, motioning to stop. This was it, no borders, no edges, no Cove, no horizon, no distractions, just aqua blue 360 degrees. As she zipped her suit, fins, mask, Wade helped put the tank on her back, checking the tether. He handed her the urn, she set Caden in a dry pak, securing it to her belt. Perched on the edge, right before the back flip into the ocean, Addie flashed Wade a great, big smile and shaka hand gesture.

Everything got quiet as she descended. Adelaide focuses on her breathing, the only sound she hears. Absolute freedom, weightless and unburdened by gravity. She has forty minutes on the tank, she will go as deep as she can. She saw Caden's fins flap in front of hers, strong, muscular hamstrings leading the way. He joked, it was the one place Adelaide let him lead. Picturing his floppy blond curls, shy face across the bow, the crooked smile in his eyes, she felt instantly beautiful. Harrison's shock and disdain when she flung open the door to a very pregnant, way too young daughter, Caden's protective arm over her shoulder. The wedding, one thousand candles, white flora abundance, twinkling lights, the yacht, her daddy's tears, Caden's promise to her father. Georgia and Max in tinted blue bathwater bubbles, "if we can't go to the sea, the girls can." Addie checked the tank, 30 minutes. It's not enough, too many memories. The operating room, Caden's eyes moist masking worried emotion, the twins came early. Stroking her sweaty brow, climbing on the gurney, wiping her forehead, "it's fine, they're perfect love. Pretty's with them." Twenty minutes, don't. I can't do this without you. Watching her husband chase his dollies, tickling, hugging, smothering, excessive kissing, was way more than promised. Caden, you held me when we lost her, crying and shaking. You squeezed my hand, drowning the sorrow. I followed you, your rock solid strength. Fifteen minutes, shit. Time babe. I have to go. Addie unhooked the dry pak, unzipped and twisted the urn. Fragments of their life danced around her in swirl formation, before he became one with the sea. You are home love, as promised. I don't care about some bucket list. I wouldn't trade one excursion for the love we shared. Not one exotic location could touch the shades we have known, the depth of our connection. Kiss Maxine a lot, tell her I'm sorry. I'm not glad you're gone, I'm happy she's with you. Take care of our funny girl. Caden, I have been so lucky. Five minutes, crap. I loved you most, even if there wasn't always time to say it. Know it.

Adelaide fins harder, pushing toward the blurry celeste outline from hazed goggles, the never-ending ocean, oxygen running low. She tugs the tether; Wade tugs back. Adelaide resurfaces removing the tank. Wade hauls it onto the boat. "That was close, missy."

"Nah, timed perfectly." Addie floated on her back, letting the water roll over her sadness. Not wanting to leave him, she needed one more minute. "I'm staying, babe. I'm finally coming home."

Crimson Waves

Adelaide knew she would return someday, the Cove was *her* heart happy home. She loved being their mother, devoted wife, hip grandmother. Jobs she excelled at, did full on. With every planned meal, birth, potty training, algebra test, fights, broken heart crushes, driving tests, princess theme birthdays, every event perfectly executed, garish, overly decorated Christmases, she grew weary, losing invisible parts. The free spirit, vibrant gypsy, sea goddess died in that house, under frozen ice, Maine snow banks. So miniscule the loss of self, she never minded. Addie had her brilliant, gorgeous daughters, smart, sexy man to fill the gaps. Summer at the beach, the grand occasion to reclaim pieces lost in the sand. Compromise was never considered, anchor weighted to her girls, family. Adelaide said nothing to Cade; he knew her heart lived in two places. Adelaide wanted them all, together. Foolish, you can't revive the dead and bury the memories. They follow you, the waves both turbulent and tubular.

Her daddy's good-humored, kindred spirit kept alive by the moments, their tender, sweet, never-ending love story. Playing tag for hours along the surf, ice cream dripping on her chin, shadow bouncing and giggly. Harry's lean, capable arms sending her soaring above the ocean, released into the shocking, cold waters screaming for more. These were her earliest, unspoiled, blissful memories.

She was ready for happy; Caden would want that.

"The sun shines through Sia." Yes, Georgia it's true. Her blinding, consuming burnt orange fire radiates from you. Adelaide lost Georgia too, when Maxine disappeared. She lost herself, leaving her daughters motherless for a time. Sia is the joy, the unbreakable nylon between them, making the precious, irreplaceable absence less intense.

Georgia arrived early, not wanting her mother to wait. Not today. 4:45. The sun says goodnight, until tomorrow. Sure bet, she almost always shines on California. The dingy pulled close to the dock, Adelaide steadied her feet as the boat rocked. Wade was taller than she thought, handsome for an old coot. He wrapped his gigantic arms around her mother, big bear hug. Adelaide rested on his shoulder for half a second. Oh no, you have got to be kidding. Georgia swung open the door and walked to the dock. Jealousy, ick, what was she feeling, threatened, don't be ridiculous. She stopped halfway to meet her mother, gazing at the water and her father.

Adelaide shook her wet mane, tied the wetsuit, hauling gear on her back. She did not look like an old woman, she looked like one of those envied, handsome women who grew more beautiful with age. Georgia recognized the pain she carried, she carried it too. Addie smiled at her fire belly, stoic, exasperating, mesmerizing, glorious grown daughter smiling back. Head crooked to the side like when she was child, perplexed and engrossed. Then her daughter did something so un-Georgia Pine, atypical, a *first*. Adelaide had to stop, steady herself on the rocking wooden planks. Georgia opened her arms to her. To greet her, meeting her halfway. The embrace lasted milliseconds, before Georgia pulled away. In between the gap lived all the words they would never share, couldn't say or take back, in the gap a daughter met her mother halfway. Georgia understood it was her turn to care for the one who had so expertly and devotedly cared for her.

They climbed in the truck, watching the sun disappear for a long while. Goodnight daddy, Georgia prayed he'd be okay without them. Wiped her eyes, twisted a strand of hair. Adelaide rested her cheek on the glass, calm and cool. She placed a palm on the dash, breaking the silence and Georgia's bad habit. She stopped, rolling her eyes. Adelaide knew the tears would come hard, over many restless nights without him, her frozen feet unable to find his to keep warm.

"I'm staying." Adelaide watched the rose blushed horizon turn mauve, go black.

"Just like that?" Georgia nodded.

"Just like that." Adelaide knew there was a whole lifetime inside the monosyllabic words. No, not quite. She was a child when she left home the first time. She had Caden to help, and a whole life with him to grow. No my darling, nothing is ever just like that. Some decisions come easier at my age. I want to die where my heart is the fullest, with the true loves of my life. She didn't say any of this to Georgia Pine, who had always needed her most.

"I want to live. Make new memories. I want you my crimson child, to have her mother, without interruption. I want to swim naked with Sia, rub off some of the glistening magic from her bare, innocent skin. I want to rock in the rocker on the screen porch, hear the maddening door slam. I want the Cove, all of her. Rich history, sun, stars, sea legacy and complete tragedy that comes from taking a chance. Love hurts, Georgia Pine. No love hurts even more. I want Harrison and Pretty to know where to find me. I want to stay close to my first, forever love. Bet you didn't know."

"Just like that, then." Georgia starts the truck. She was beginning.

Opalescence

When the letter arrived from Paris, X was reeling in bed, grieving the loss of Georgia Pine, the days spent in excellent company. Harrison and her descendants were not just words on paper. To her they were family, made the loneliness tolerable. She sat up in bed blowing her nose, tossing the tissue onto the wad pile on the floor, mountain peak high. Intrigued, Opal normally sent postcards. X ripped the seam carefully, a letter fell out with a photo neatly folded inside. Opal and a lanky boy with long, brown locks, blue eyes and a puppy were smiling and waving at her, le Pompidou the backdrop. Opal did not share her smile willingly, when she did it was Opalescence, luminescence, portrait worthy.

The note, a few short paragraphs, was long enough to pull X out of bed.

Dear X,

I did it! I made it to Paris, the city of yellow lights Harrison described so vividly. I keep my copy of The Vast Landscape close, in my purse with the unopened test result. The pages loose from the binding, a supersize elastic holds my personal bible together. J'adore Paris X, I'm sorry Harry felt so alone. Exploring the 'glass couvert' secret gardens, ornate floor tiling, the tack tack sound of heels passing by. 11th century antique streets, the absorbed history. Rue Dussoubs, Rue Montorgueil cobblestone streets, warm crepes with butter and sugar, le Marais, Rue Saint- Denis, the Quai de la Megisserie, pet shops along the

Seine, hundreds upon hundreds of bookstalls. The Berger de Pyrenees tan and white puppy beaming from behind the glass. You would love the Bouquinistes X, antiquarian and used booksellers, rolling R's, Montmartre, St Germaine des Pres. I won't bore you with the scenery; I'm no writer.

I met a boy, the one in the picture. An artist, painter with an Irish brogue so thick I'm just beginning to decipher it. I told him everything. My mom, the crap statistics, Huntington's, the decision to never have kids. You know what he did, purchased that most adorable, cutest, smartest puppy behind the glass. We named him Hopper. "NO dog tuition, think of the money we'll save." I decided if I'm going to die, I'm going to live the fifty percent guarantee, to hell with the other half.

Hope you're having an excellent day, X.
Stellar. Au revoir.
Bisous,
Opal

Comings and Goings

Stellar. X propped the photo on the TV table using copious amounts of prescription bottles as a frame. She was tired, exhausted. She was tired of her self-imposed limitations, tired by the routine, tired of the hate, blame, self-pity. This was not living, no; these four walls needed a fresh coat of paint. Something cheerful and inviting, not the safe muddy brown she was used to. Bossy was late. X showered yesterday, she would dress herself and get in the chair. Surprise Bossy. X miscalculated the distance to the chair ending up on the carpet. Ouch, that hurt. Laughing like a hyena, uncontrollable snorts and howls kept right on coming. The bells. Bossy came around the corner heading straight for the bed, package in hand, perplexed. Her laser focus didn't spot X on the floor, eyes trained on the bed. "Um, *hello*."

"Oh my GOD, what the hell?" Bossy sits on the carpet beside X, resting a hand on her shoulder, afraid to touch her. "I'm calling 911. Where does it hurt?"

"I'm fine, stupid. Overshot the chair, can you please get it. Sooner than later, my ass is chaffing." X turns her head, moving her arms, hands, fingers. "All good, see."

"Little shit. Scared the bejesus…okay, let's roll." Bossy positions the chair as close as possible, locking the brakes. Reaching under her arms, looks at X, "ready," uses all her body weight thrusting X back into the chair to safety.

"What's that," giggling, nodding at the package, guessing what's inside.

"The reason I was late Fancy Pants, post office needed a signature."

"You can't call me that, you're Bossy Pants," teasing. Bossy wasn't bossy at all, she was her loyal caregiver, tough, decent, companion, true friend, the lovely person who never quit on her. With a stubborn streak, and one hell of a lot of patience.

"I want to go outside on the porch."

"Are you sure…um, ok," Bossy's eyelids blinking at Mach Five. "Of course, breakfast?"

X shakes her head, looking at the double doors. "You have to get the screwdriver, otherwise I won't fit. A Kind bar and Vitamin water, out there."

"Hold up." Bossy heads to the kitchen, hands trembling, petrified, cursing under her breath. She opens the tool drawer and shakes her head. Bossy has dropsy, the screwdriver, water and Kind bar slip through her fingers. Thud. She quickly bends down, scooping up the items, trying to play it cool. The last time X went outside, it did not go well. It was a fucking disaster; Bossy's hands tremble. She grabs a broom sweeps the porch, fluffs the cushion on the rocker, sets a TV table with snacks, stalling. Xanax is by the bed, cell phone in her back pocket.

X waits, realizing she's spent her whole life waiting. What's five more minutes?

Bossy gazes at her with panicked eyes, doing a shitty job of hiding her I'm not freaking the fuck out face. "Let's do this."

X blinks. Bossy gets behind her, patting the top of her shoulder, wheeling the chair towards the wide-open space, expecting X to scream.

X closes her eyes, grasping the open door frame so hard her knuckles turn violet. Bossy wants to pull her back inside where it's safe, she does not move. Bossy was there the first time, she understands the weight bearing decision. The tears roll down her face, quickly wiping them with her torn sweatshirt sleeve. She waits, hands gripped tight around the arms of the chair. X inhales deep, releasing her cramped fingers. Closing her eyes she breathes in the atmosphere, mowed lawns, the smell of fresh paint. When she opens them, she's temporarily blinded by the sunlight. Overwhelmed, she takes a minute to find her footing which is a cliché and ridiculous. X doesn't have feet she must rely on her senses to walk again. On the front porch, X spots the masking tape stain on the worn beige siding, still there from a long forgotten Christmas. The black railing is chipped, flecks of paint scattered on the frayed gray carpet. The massive white pillars look smaller than she remembered. Through the eyes of a five-year-old, everything looks delicious and feels like a carnival. The evergreens were massive, overgrown and in need of a good pruning. X's eyes slightly out of focus, adjust to the daylight, fresh air and her new surroundings. Bossy sits in the rocker beside her. Funny, they didn't look like the wicker rockers she remembered and gave to Harry at the Cove. This wicker was cracked, one chair missing an arm and ready to be tossed. This was not scary at all, just drastically different. X glances up and down the street, which has been paved and repaved so many times there are no traces of what happened. Only one neighbor remains from childhood, an old woman now, children grown with kids of their own. The houses aren't homes anymore, no longer dwellings of pride, filled with family and love. Kids she doesn't recognize play in the streets, trucks and cars are parked haphazardly in the road. Weird, some man she doesn't know waves at her from across the street. She's sad to see the foreclosure signs, unkempt, decrepit shacks had taken over her childhood wonderland. So much time wasted, so much time passed, so much time spent worrying and hiding. Why did I wait so long? "I'll be in the kitchen," Bossy gets up, understanding she's okay and needs a minute.

X feels her mother's presence sitting in the rocker, saying nothing. Basking in the light of her daughter, respecting her silence. She hears her mother's raspy, smoker's voice, "No matter where I go, no matter where I am Frankie, you are going to be just fine. Everything is going to be fine."

X flinched at the sound of her birth name. That day, the day she was sliced open, blood gushing guts and insides exposed everyone was screaming, "FRANKIE!!!!" Her mother flew up the street howling Frankie, over and over. The EMTS trying to save her unsalvageable parts, "Frankie stay with us. Frankie, come on." Months in the hospital, nurses in and out, coma, surgeries, the name bracelet, she could not escape the nightmare Frankie was.

"Frankie." X blurted it out, no monsters, ghosts, motorcycle thieves came for her other half.

She was very much alive. Frankie bent down to open the brown bubble envelope. Two Arc copies inside, gently touching the cover beaming. The indescribable feeling of accomplishment, pride, this was *her* heart happy home. The book of *Georgia Pine.* She cracked the spine, a thick solid spine built on love that could not be broken. Frankie flipped the pages, the dedication.

Because of You, Opal.

A twinge of elation consumed her, followed by regret.

Because of you, Opal.

Opal had no idea of the validity of the words and all that they had meant. *Because of you, Opal,*

X trusted the words and Harrison's world again. *Because of you, Opal*, she brushed her teeth and got out of bed. *Because of you, Opal,* the jagged scars, eggplant tint, wrinkles and gnarly veins on her stumps looked less grotesque. *Because of you, Opal,* the self-hatred felt less like hate. *Because of you, Opal,* X no longer hid behind a false identity. She was no longer an acronym, anonymous, the invisible shut-in relearning to speak and hear the sound of her God given name. X and Frankie were the same, she could no longer compartmentalize the five-year-old pain. *Because of you, Opal,* after decades of hiding in place behind other people's faces and names, she longed for a space she could belong. *Because of you, Opal,* X pitied herself a little less. *Because of you, Opal,* born sparkly, fire beautiful and quartz strong. *Because of you, Opal,* hope crept in over the decades, at first the inaudible whisper and then the piercing megaphone that would not be ignored. *Because of you, Opal,* X found bravery, resilience and self-love in a shallow breath. *Because of You, Opal,* wonder, acceptance, blinding faith and choosing life carry on. X did not know one letter from the naïve quiet warrior would be the catalyst that would save her life.

The Vast Landscape was the start to Opal's beginnings. *Georgia Pine* was Frankie's reason to go on. With every *come what may* ending, follows a *like it or not* beginning. It's how gracefully you live, the comings and goings that count. Harrison was Frankie's brazen, bold, raw, chaotic creation, the lines so blurred at times they became one. The fantasy so alive in her mind, no one could erase. The words, she owned them. "*Making memories babe, making memories. Harrison is gone, but no longer lost. Harry is home, set free.*" Frankie couldn't say goodbye to her best self, but it was time for Harrison to be going.

Frankie desperately wanted to believe half a whole was a fine place to start. No, a *stellar* one.

Frankie and Sia?...maybe, who knows. She didn't. One double oak door with jalousies at a time. Sitting on that porch, Frankie felt less scared. Neither memories, demons nor ghosts could hurt her. She set the past carefully by the side of the road.

"Fine, Frankie. *You* are going to be just fine." For the first time, Frankie watched the little girl, her five-year-old self with freckles and the sweetest carefree happy face, dance twirl and skip through the streets without envy.

CAST OF CHARACTERS

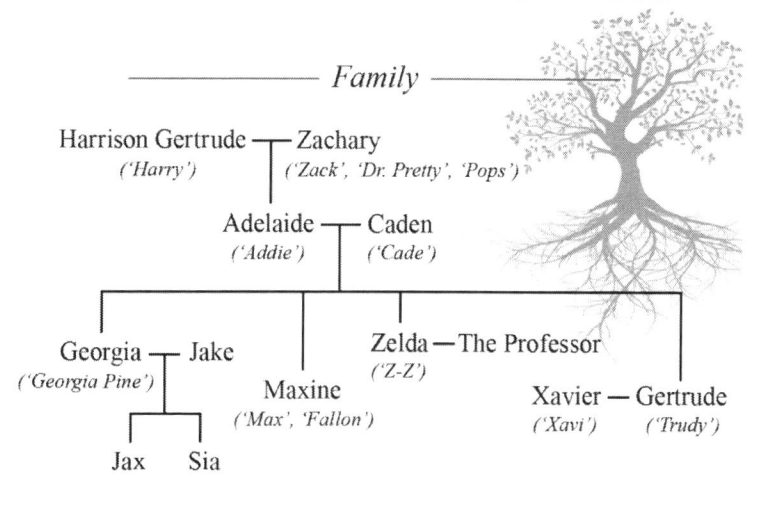

Family

Harrison Gertrude — Zachary
('Harry') *('Zack', 'Dr. Pretty', 'Pops')*

Adelaide — Caden
('Addie') *('Cade')*

Georgia — Jake
('Georgia Pine')

Maxine
('Max', 'Fallon')

Zelda — The Professor
('Z-Z')

Xavier — Gertrude
('Xavi') *('Trudy')*

Jax   Sia

Friends

Miss Bossy
('Bossy Pants')

Miss Barbara

Elizabeth
('Liz', 'Lizzie')

Tucker

Opal
('Opal Jett', 'Seven')

'Dash'
('el Stinko', Son of Tucker)

Mettus Thaddeus
('M.T.')

Jenny
(Harry's Assistant)

Eveleen
(M.T.'s Grand-Daughter)

Sofia & Katia
(Harry's BFFs)

ACKNOWLEDGEMENTS

I'd like to thank my mother, Ellen May Hickey Cioffa for knowing precisely when to push and when to pull. I'm grateful for her unwavering support in life and during the writing process of this book. She is the who, how and where *(see, it fits!)* that has shaped my life. To my brother, Tom, for being the most insightful creative person I know. All the cool that lives in me and *Georgia Pine* brushed off from you. Terry Hickey, thank you for the loving attention and thought-FULL editing. Your pink pen, pencil, and keen comments made the manuscript a well-polished novel. To my father for his love and guiding light, you were a king among men. Without him, I would not have experienced the meaning of profound love.

Kara Moran, thank you for every call, text, for never quitting. For challenging me to push a little bit farther, and always choosing the harder, more satisfying route. Ride the wave I'm right behind you. Malena Holcomb, thank you for being the sister of my soul, protector, yin and yang kindred spirit. The book exists because you do, thank you for being the keeper of the words. Gianni Ghidini, thank you for your artistic excellence and raw talent.

To Sue Cioffa and the girls. Thank you for the forever support with the book and more importantly, in life.

My gratitude for their early and forever support goes to Julie Davidow, Felice Pappas, Patricia and Giuseppe Piazzi, Tim Quinn, Suzanne Hai, Dr. Parker, Patricia Nash, ILIV staff, Dina Schwartz, Kathleen Grace, Patrizia Ferrante, Mark Blickley, Rebecca Batties and Downtown Books Publishing.

Dr. Laurie Beth Hickey. Thank you for being both precious and precocious. I write with my heart full of you.

Thanks to Lupita, my furball shadow love who never leaves my side and smiles each time she greets me. No matter the day, mood or the weather.

To the orbs and the power of a beautiful chaotic mind I thank you.

ABOUT THE AUTHOR

Jacqueline Cioffa was an international model for 17 years and celebrity makeup artist. She lived and worked in Europe for a decade, appearing in ads for Armani, Moschino, and Hermes. Living with manic depression, Jacqueline is an advocate for mental health awareness. She's an observer, dog lover, crystal collector, essayist and film lover who's traveled the world. She is co-author of *Model Citi Zen, the guide* and has published numerous prose pieces in various literary magazines. Jacqueline is featured in *Brainstorms, the Anthology* by Little Episodes.

Her acclaimed debut novel *The Vast Landscape* is available on Amazon.com.

Links:
http://choff777.wordpress.com
http://bit.ly/vastlandscape

Made in the USA
Middletown, DE
01 March 2015